LEXICON OF AFFINITIES

First published by Charco Press 2025
Charco Press Ltd., Office 59, 44-46 Morningside Road, Edinburgh
EH10 4BF

First published in Spanish as *Léxico de afinidades*

This book was published with funding from the IDA Programme from
Uruguay XXI and the Ministry of Education & Culture of Uruguay / Este
libro fue publicado gracias al Programa IDA de Uruguay XXI y el MEC.

A CIP catalogue record for this book is available from the British Library.

ISBN: 9781913867591
e-book: 9781913867607

www.charcopress.com

Edited by Fionn Petch
Cover design by Pablo Font
Typeset by Laura Jones-Rivera
Proofread by Fiona Mackintosh

Ida Vitale

LEXICON OF AFFINITIES

Translated by
Sean Manning

CHARCO PRESS

For the three beloved clans who opened their tents to me:
the Maggi Silva Vilas, in Uruguay; the Mutis Miracles
and Villegas Medinas, in Mexico.
For Aurelio Major, faithful illusionist.
And for Enrique, always.

... like a gust of things
scattered at random,
the beautiful cosmos...
Lucretius

Lucretius
– ancient name –
with the poetic sound of things
in fixed whirlwinds...
Enrique Casaravilla Lemos

Meaning is a fish that cannot
last long out of its turbid waters.
Jean Dubuffet

... lexicon / in order of combat...
Guillermo Carnero

STATEMENT OF INTENTIONS

The world is chaotic and, fortunately, difficult to classify, but chaos, matter susceptible to wondrous transformation, presents the temptation of order, as any theogony can demonstrate. We live in search of the best system to organize it all, to understand it at least. Until that one irrefutable order comes along, the most innocent option is alphabetical. Its vastness can resemble the chaos it looks to substitute. So I will limit it according to my affinities, selecting the lexicon that crystallizes, arbitrarily, around each letter: not all of them, only those words that sing to me. But a song is both a river and a net. Words mutually frolic, conspire, float, they are suicidal, dynastic, migratory, their every roar far from the inertia. They do not expect us, ephemeral, standing on the wayside, to think them eternal, or that we can, ignorant of where we are, know our eventual destination following their lead. They are content if we, obeying some of their intentions, avail ourselves of what they propose, commensurate with our thirst and our glass.

A

abracadabra

To begin with, magic:
abraxas, abrasax, abracadabra.
But can
ce beau mot pour guérir la fièvre
abscind all desolating fires,
craters that do not spout their lava?

advance

We advance only when the sounding line strikes in
the deeps.

affectation

I discovered Mallarmé's 'Brise marine' as an
adolescent and was drenched by the conclusive
force of its famed first verse: *La chair est triste, hélas!
et j'ai lu tous les livres.* At the time, I knew nothing
about the sadness of the flesh as he understood it.
I enjoyed the sunlit wind, nice walks, my favorite
flavors. I could perhaps sense certain metaphysical

3

melancholies, even moral ones, but none that were physical. With a large family that had been steadily dismantling and a paternal grandmother who regularly kindled the oral altar of our departed, death was not easy to forget and occasioned melancholic states. I did not lack for examples of injustice and cowardice provided by one relative who, despite our many decent and sorely missed domestic dead, still remained among the living, undoubtedly due to some celestial oversight. It was logical then that I had the rasping suspicion that adult life deals us an intolerable duplicity, as well as other mysteries, and that I erected an ethical scaffolding against eventual collapses. But none of this justified the obsessive modulation of that verse which set corporeal sadness to the hypnotic rhythm of its two crisp hemistiches. As for the second of these, in those days I squandered my reading, devouring more than I could assimilate. When evening fell on the conclusion of that day's book, the hours until bedtime felt like an eternity. What was I to do with those recently revealed lives? They were my real world. Once I closed the cover on characters whose dreams, sorrows, and misadventures I felt brimming inside me, it was desolating not to be able to talk about them, to find myself surrounded by beings with no interest in that artificial paradise that had just gone dark. But, of course, I had not *read every book*. Quite the opposite, my greatest happiness came from my certainty that they awaited me in infinite numbers. I had been promised as much. When I finished reading Thomas Mann's *The Magic Mountain*, I felt for the first time the sorrow of having glimpsed a world that will always be beyond us and whose revelation was a decisive and singular experience. I shared this with the poet Carlos Sábat Ercasty, our literature professor at the time, who assured me there were other books to come which I was also going to admire. Not without my doubts, I chose to believe him. Later I would discover that writing was inexhaustible, that *every book* was, would always be part of the immediate future. Many years had to pass, years that take as much as they bring, for my obsession with new books and new authors to subside. Rereading those 'few but learned' works was joy enough. Mallarmé's truth was therefore not my truth, and yet that verse and I became intertwined, forming a bond tighter than any tying me to other books that I read passionately and sometimes immediately forgot. One day I was amazed to learn that Mallarmé was barely thirty-three years old at the moment of that skeptical verse. He had undoubtedly not read every book either, and his flesh, though sad, had already contributed to the birth of a daughter.

anaphoric
>Present that refers
>through more murk
>than light, to the past,
>*sépulcre solide où gît tout ce qui nuit,*[1]
>in whose infinite caverns
>awaits our memory
>of how,
>>deluded,
>>>we dreamt of the future.

---

[1] S. Mallarmé.

Aquaster

According to Paracelsus, an antifeminist, as was certainly also his reincarnation Faust, there is a fissure at the back of the woman's head and in the forehead of the man through which both receive the Aquaster or spiritual principle (a humid, medieval precursor of the unconscious). This entrance or connection functions as a telepathic, necrocomic antenna. Women, poorly oriented, are receptive to diabolical hordes. Men, to life's higher spirits. Thanks to this principle, women found themselves dedicated to the meticulous and malicious organization of wars during their time out from more obvious tasks like witchcraft and commerce. Meanwhile, men filled with generous spirits wove and composed the precious, yellow and blood red paintings of the Holy Inquisition, invented the wholesome ghettos and their even more wholesome liquidation, gunpowder and the atomic bomb, dictatorships, military interventions, historical misrepresentations, the decimation of the whales, the chemical poisoning of the oceans, and other means of survival. And antifeminism, including the kind practised without being formulated.

Artemis

I assume my ancient labor.
I attempt the verdure of dawn.
To frigid waters I return.
Artemis in words I quiver.

aspidistra

If under the pretext of returning the water to its empty pitcher, I devoted myself to that mixture of mournful dredging and sentimental delight that one's memories of childhood and adolescence often become under the literary name of *memoirs*, then I should dare title them: *In the Shadow of the Flowerless Aspidistras.* They welcomed me each day after school, multiplied throughout the corners, on shelves, on tables, on balconies, abusive and fanged. Only dust tempered the somber green of their large tough leaves. In the first house, the house that I loved, there were other plants and even trees that let me ignore the aspidistras and their wretched air of neutral doctor's office décor. But a decision not approved by me moved us to a centrally located second-floor apartment – everything about it was high, its ceilings, its doors – where the aspidistras usurped every dangerously arid space. The supple ferns loathed, as did I, the skylights through which the cold or heat descended in a harsh light without sky or nuance, and so they shriveled. The exotic ylang-ylang and the prodigious perfume of its fragile, drooping yellow flowers – a blend of rose and violet – stayed behind like a beautiful improvement in the garden I had lost, like an inexplicable sense of overpowering nostalgia, like an appointment postponed for half a lifetime, fulfilled unexpectedly and fleetingly one January morning in a tall frozen garden in Rome when the call of an aroma, elusive at first, recognized by my heart before my mind, caused me to run toward the hidden second row of rust-colored bushes. I would encounter them again later during other Italian winters. But the aspidistras… The aspidistras crowded against the now shriveled and brittle pluvial creepers. Dazzling azaleas, a lavish flower in Uruguayan winters, lilies of the valley, and delicate palms came along like a gift. The aspidistras were unfazed, like a rugged camel looking at a delicate gazelle transplanted to the desert. They knew that the joy and regard intended for those colorful and attractively shaped apparitions would wither once they were swallowed by that vortex consuming everything iridescent, porcelain flowers, peacock feathers, hummingbirds. The monsters dominated, but... they were tinged with sorrow despite themselves. I had to fight against them like I did the order and silence of adults, against dark wallpapers, closed drawers, the sordidness of a certain individual. And when one day those graceless plants, every one of them, produced a surreptitious flower, tiny and violet at soil level, I hated them even more. Regardless how botany may feel about it, I have erased that accidental and never repeated flower, which they were free to offer, at long last, and which I was free to deem superfluous to their ecclesiastical severity.

August (and the Perseids)

Faintly imagined,
fleetingly radiant,
you must remain, year after year,
a blind woman attempting
to create herself in a mirror.

autumn

Rust-covered parterres, sparse roses, rickles of ragged branches, embers on the brink of extinction, ruins reduced to the passion for rebirth when it is over; also the faithful perfume of the last flowerings, the first expirations. All of this borne by that somewhat cool wind on skin slightly weary of the sun, somewhat warm on skin that begins to resist the oncoming cold. Autumn is tinted with the perfections we attribute to summer, the resentments with which we surround the winter, a linear (not cyclical) renaissance (not modern) vision of time. But we, renaissance and not modern, continue to believe that everything has been organized for us, for our glory or our grief. The profusion and authority of one spectrum of colors over another, that is, rivalry, struggle. We are the center, everything concerns us and this struggle, and this destruction is carried out according to us. Or are we entirely extraneous, just another element in a game of final stages? In this case we cling to the pleasures of the start of autumn and ask the season to linger for it is too beautiful to lose or to risk not being on earth next year, to await its return.

B

Baltic

The heart dodges probabilities. Solitude, like a useless string, sways softly in the white night.

Bayley, Edgar

Heidegger, no doubt in need of hope, once said that when we think about someone, what comes to us is not a partial image of that person but their entire self. With this same hope, I follow a drawing being sketched by my memory, and Edgar Bayley is again with me, still alive in his city where we met him decades, many decades, ago. But that drawing is more like the edge of an intriguing void. This page is more like the mold of a story. The vast emptiness fills with skies, books, characters, real people, their glories, and their trifles. And with Edgar's poetry also and appearances by his unforgettable Pi Torrendell.

We encountered him by chance, a chance he accepted and guided. We were in Buenos Aires walking not far from a public library where Raúl Gustavo Aguirre worked. Enrique wanted to thank him for a kind review he had written some time earlier about a book of his, so we decided to stop in. When we asked for him, an immense blond man emerged and for several seconds we could not understand a word he was saying. A large mustache muddled his ghastly diction even more. Two things eventually became clear: Aguirre was not there because 'he had gone to a funeral, possibly his own', and that this was Edgar Bayley.

Certain names make us think of pseudonyms. I had sometimes assumed that his was one. It had in part been his choice. He had a first surname, Maldonado, from his father, and he had a brother. Looking to the future, they decided to divide the two surnames between them, like a piece of land or an inheritance. He told us: 'We all assumed the poet, that is, me, was going to be the famous one of the family. I took Bayley. Now he is the (famous) architect Tomás Maldonado.' Silence underscored his: 'And I...'

The coffee we had together was not enough. He insisted we join him for dinner at his house the following evening. There we would meet Alicia Dujovne Ortiz, his wife at the time. It was reasonable to imagine that if two strangers like us were worthy of annexation, then the gates to those heavens must have been opened quite often. Perhaps Edgar handed out surprise invitations with greater regularity than what the seraphic patience of a housewife with inherent chores not delegated, a daughter to care for, and a life's work to write could tolerate.

The dinner was unforgettable. Preceded by free-flowing wine, it began with four monumental oven-roasted onions, each one prominent on each plate, each one its own antemural. As I followed the conversation, I was nervously occupied with dismantling mine, trying to make it appear smaller, but nature and its characteristic efficacy had managed to concentrate an enormous amount of onion in the smallest possible space. My efforts only managed to transform it, now entirely out of hand, into a furious and ever more visible mountain rising up before me. It is not that I dislike onions, but I see them as an accompaniment, a garnish. We get along when the culinary arts tame their natural violence. That was not the case. That one was wild like an Amazon and powerful enough to abolish the rest of the menu, most likely normal, from my memory.

Memories suffer from anamorphosis depending on how you look at them. How might Alicia have remembered that dinner? And Edgar? They were separated sometime after.

We bumped into Alicia again in Paris, this time without onions. She was working, writing, always good humored in her approach to life. At a conference in Mexico with some of my compatriots in attendance, a person whose style was nothing like Alicia's, perfectly comfortable in its grace, looked at her with the same inadequacy as I had her bulb years before. Between one encounter and another, we recaptured her humor in her books. I admired the writer in her who could turn the hostile elements of domesticity and life into text, and I understood her cuisine. We were thrilled when *El buzón de la esquina* became *La bonne Pauline* and earned an Italian edition as well. And when her family found themselves fantastically mixed up with none other than Christopher Columbus in a novel that earned a French edition. She had another book about Eva Duarte, but I could not rhyme Columbus with Perón, not even in Spanish; for me that part of history was someone else's misfortune, and I never got around to reading it.

We never saw Edgar again. For long obvious years we did not visit Buenos Aires. We were told that he was sometimes spotted in Punta del Este, in Uruguay. We heard through mutual friends about a new or rediscovered partner. Enrique tracked him down, found his phone number, and during a short trip across the river, left him a message shortly before our departure. When Edgar called, we had already gone. Time passed. We were in Berkeley. Our paths did not cross. He had just been there, also invited, leaving his very distinctive echo in that circumspect university life.

One day we returned to Buenos Aires, so close and yet so far. The sadness of many deaths weighed heavily on us: José Bianco, Enrique Pezzoni, María Emilia Avellaneda, the architect Valerio Peluffo. Valerio and his wife Olga Orozco had once been in Mexico having lunch at our house. He was being unusually quiet when I noticed a celadon green spot next to his fingernail. After subjecting it to an immediate treatment of warm salt water to cause a 'maturation', in accordance with long-standing domestic traditions, we felt a professional eye was needed. It was Sunday. Since the father of our neighbor Pedro Serrano was a surgeon, his mother was able to point us toward a nearby clinic. There they approved of my treatment but sent both Valerio and his finger to bed with blood pressure *tous azimuts*. The infected finger became secondary, though it was perhaps the first sign of a circulatory problem that two years later would take from us the most angelical and adamant lover of Raphael paintings we have ever known.

Someone told us again that Edgar was very sick, but this news was now customary. Another time in Buenos Aires, and also as per custom, Enrique phoned him. 'Yeah, I wasn't well,' he said. 'It's lucky you called today! A month ago, I decided to stop eating. A couple of days ago, a few charitable souls brought me empanadas. They almost killed me, but I'm doing better now. I'm off to see the doctor. Come by tomorrow.' The next day, we phoned as we were leaving for his house. A nurse answered and said that they were taking him to the hospital at that very moment. And hung up. Where? None of our mutual acquaintances knew. We were leaving the next day. He lived little more than a week. Now we are visited by the ghost of conversations we never had.

What should you do when you are essentially a romantic but live in a time and place where the avant-garde has taken root and there is, on the one hand, an affiliated surrealist movement with prestigious names and journals, and, on the other, the Madí group (dialectical materialism), made up mostly of visual artists who are also theorists and affirmers? Be Bayley.

Bayley loathed the fate of a verse he had written in his youth: '*Es infinita esta riqueza abandonada*' (Infinite is this abandoned wealth). Any author who discovers that every reader memorizes the same verse, that every anthologist routinely chooses the same poem, would suffer as Bayley did. If he suspected he was about to be assailed by his own words, these ones in particular, like someone anticipating a blatant aggression, he would rush to cast the first stone: the verse. There was no use telling him that critical memory's compulsive predilections often depend not on consent or the profundity of the chosen matter but on the elasticity of its application. Its condition as an open metaphor takes precedence. But he wanted, rightfully so, to be faithful to the rest of his works.

Among those works, we cannot forget the short texts produced by the fantastic Pi Torrendell and other prose that engages in the same state of incongruous grace. Pi Torrendell is an imaginary character who sometimes shares situations with real characters, such as Francisco Madariaga, Edgar's notable poet friend and deceased accomplice in literary adventures. In everyday settings and in pleasant contradiction, Pi Torrendell finds himself embroiled in bizarre situations that affect us through the precise impact of an absurd formula ('you must have') or an adjective ('gothic'), transmitters of ridiculousness and excess in this brief example I can offer:

The card: I enter an office at the Department of Scientific Investigations. My brother has entrusted me with a task. I have to see one of their personnel and somehow participate in an investigation. I am greeted by an employee who asks for my card.

I tell him I do not have one. 'You must have one,' he answers. And he shows me his own card printed with gothic lettering. 'One like this, you see?' I nod, put the card in my pocket, and leave. On the street, a woman of a certain age stops me and looks at me with a mixture of amazement, happiness, and sorrow. It happens that I very much remind her of her deceased husband.

I feel confused and to get away, I hand her the card with gothic lettering that they had just given me.

bilberry

At a moment when I was navigating my way by petrified and refutable memory through the hazy details of past readings, with no library on hand to come to my aid, the Royal Spanish Academy's denigrated and slow-moving dictionary shed light after a span of years on a phrase from Ramón del Valle-Inclán. Quoted as a comical absurdity by Rafael Alberti in his *Imagen primera de…*, it remained so for me as I awaited further explanation. The younger poet is listening to the elder writer describe the glories of the Pincio Gardens in Rome. As they walk by several myrtle bushes, Valle-Inclán identifies them as a plant used to prepare an exquisite compote. I also wondered: myrtle compote? I told myself that the writer's imagination was not limited to the multiple and contradictory accounts of his missing arm but invaded the domain of the kitchen as well.

Many years later, after inspiring adventitious promenades through the dictionary, from one word to another, the search for an evasive clarification transformed the fantastical myrtle berry jam into that yuletide jam made with bilberries, *Vaccinium myrtillus*, *arándano* in Spanish. Everything was falling into place, or into jars, if you prefer. But I could not stop thinking about the nearly insurmountable confusion that arises when we talk about plants and birds. Do I know what the boxwood is or not? Is Hudson's ecstasy at the singing calandra lark a close relative of my ecstasy at the singing *cenzontle*, *sinsonte*, or mockingbird? How do they refer to the timid and clever *ratonera* or wren in other lands and languages? Confusion of names, confusion of attributes, like what for many makes Greek mythology so discouraging, its gods changing characteristics and duties from one region to another,

17

one invocation to another, no one knowing if they are in the presence of the same Heracles, the same Apollo, the same Venus.

Such imprecisions create chasms. Rejections and aversions form at their edges, to the same degree that the majority of mortals – and the occasional immortal or aspirant to that academic condition – are increasingly less familiar with the words stored inside dictionaries. It is not hard to imagine how nationalist inclinations can be exacerbated to disagree on the realities designated by names like hibiscus, apricot, bergamot, or mango; and how some annotated editions of texts renowned for the richness of their writing oscillate between evading the problem and offering absurd or ill-defined solutions.

bird

Faraway a train thunders forth
discharging a deathly sound,
various voices roil the wind,
a bark, all alone, takes a bite.

But a bird sings and all that
is not bird starts to recede.
Bird-river, dendriform light,
spoken light, precious particle,

master of its time within time,
all glory to its smallness.
I exist more if it spins
this cocoon of sonorous silk.

birth

Everything that converges, dense, and condenses to devise a birth determines its prolongation in an infinite echo that resounds until the death – perhaps beyond? – of the signatory who enters the world. Zodiac signs, terrestrial signs, spoken signs, ritual signs are usually preserved in the memories of others, coated by the luster of another's generous gaze. But there is a diverse factory from which these others emerge: the one the lone individual constructs alone if she lacks the assistance, albeit meager and flawed, of those who experienced her childhood. Alongside distracted third parties, she imagines from inside the density of time, which nevertheless seems empty to her. She casts desperate buckets down a deep dark well whose walls, under the clanging metal, sometimes ignite shreds of strange mosses. She struggles against the barricades that pretend to let themselves be breached and then offer lightning flashes of dazzling light or compact blackness. Intimacy forms between her intimate ear and the dissolution of concreteness. If nothing behind her responds, if an indecipherable nebula shuts every possible door, she stills the tuning fork that could sustain true music. She will only be able to follow the childhoods of others, those who are just beginning to live their adventure, those who will soon disregard any witnesses until, now adults themselves, they lament the absence of that mirror where they could see the reflection of their own years of this invention, this occurrence, this unique and carefree inner freedom.

boat

At night I never know if I should make my way toward sleep or wait for it to come to me. Because I have yet to master this, I am faced with a routine of restless insomnia. My stillness as I skeptically lie waiting for rest to arrive leads me to awaken images which I attribute with reflective powers. I materialize a nearly slumbering stream, green and shaded, and in it the essential feature, a small boat with its oars crossed waiting for me. I always see it from shore. Maybe sleep overcomes me before I try to climb in. Maybe I am afraid that when I do, the inevitable rocking will wake me up completely. Or, since I cannot swim and thus my aquatic enthusiasms are purely platonic, it is possible that some still-repressive unconscious is tasked with keeping me safe even though my aspirations would certainly go no further than relaxing, stretched out in the boat (I provide myself with a pillow) in the calm shade of a tree. This too I materialize effortlessly: it is a willow, the tree best suited to this privileged, front (and cool) row situation. I never trouble myself with completing the horizons of this landscape, unnecessary since I am searching for an intimate, private space. In reality, what I have created is the magnified detail of a large and meticulous painting. I never concentrate hard enough to multiply the minutiae. If we want to sleep, fixing our attention on something that begins to interest us is counterproductive. But we know that when we focus on that small patch of sky, held in place by foliage or hazy towers, or on the wildflowers or the dog or the bird that a painter brings to life in some corner of their work to eliminate an emptiness, that corner, as if by some act of vindictive magic, usurps the importance that should correspond to the Virgin, a young woman with unicorn, a young woman in real life, or whatever the painter's diligent imagination has chosen as the center. The essential object then is the boat. I call it this, not a skiff, and in doing so I grant it not a detailed background, but indeed certain legendary references. I have never added an oarsman to it, undoubtedly because a human being would not bring more peace – my essential quest – and would attempt to fulfill their duties by propelling boat and passenger somewhere. The boat seems to encapsulate since who knows when a thirst for irresponsibility and secrecy, for pleasant silent flotation, for leisure without ennui, for discoveries without disturbance. The climate that surrounds it is free from changes in temperature, mosquitos, frights; it does admit birdsong. My boat has the essential virtue of being in an unreal space, accessible only to the benevolent and from where I could, reassured, welcome the world, piece by piece, forgive it its depravities, reconcile with it, elevate it to the level of my hopefulness, improbable upon waking.

boredom

I am not unacquainted with the existence of overwhelming individuals who glided through childhood without a minute of boredom, light-hearted, without an afternoon of cottony interlude, indistinguishable from other identical afternoons, like one dish of thick, sweet semolina at snack time from the next identical dish, like one day's protest from yesterday's and tomorrow's, like one defeat from another from another... I know there are overwhelming, indulged individuals who enjoyed the proximity of an abundance of adults, multiple or in turn, occupied in entertaining them with the patience of their pedagogical vitality, brothers and sisters or close cousins who, not without self-interest but useful just the same, shared their time, accelerating it. I am familiar with those swindled individuals, even if they decorously conceal themselves, obscurely aware of being a crack in a surface that should be taut, and perhaps say and even believe that they do not want to overwhelm us with the exemplarity of their adherence to the model of Happy Childhood. I repeat, I am not unacquainted with them, but I look upon them with slight apprehension. Potential boredom is a source of knowledge and countless inventions; it is the desert where the mirage, better than life, unexpectedly appears; imaginary water, a palm tree laden with dates and delusive shade existing in the pure air of our willingness for wonder. A certain sense of melancholy, a few drops of controlled hatred, which Baudelaire exalts as a source of poetry, can flow from those days of woolly tedium and project themselves into an unanticipated creative moment today.

In childhood, time weighs heavily because we do not know how to interrupt its massive avalanche, impose the proper cosmetic that will sweeten its gaze, drive back its continuous substance that will one day irreparably envelop us all. We have not yet discovered Death and have not begun the fight against nullification which will consume our lives. Is that fight not the opposite of boredom? Until we initiate it, we have wasted our time. Let us devote a minor deity to boredom, if the Greeks have not already.

Borges

In the Borgesian forest light is dark,
all that is black holds inside it the white,
the white that is myriad and the lone
solar color, even the tragic black
that unfortunate souls will know as
the tormented absence of inner light.

He watched maliciousness and force go by,
calm in his allegiances and patience.
He wandered labyrinths, devised mirrors,
zahirs and infinite libraries,
quiet inside a center of wisdom
ever shifting with blistering speed.

Of other paths, of no certain nation,
of powerful and long forgotten gods
was the memory where they were reborn.
He revered by perceiving, distinct from
the echo and cast of banalities.
Nothing in him dies, if we rebegin.

breeze

A breeze is a mysterious blaze
that kindles your skin with its touch.

Bruckner

Between the flight of the bumblebee
and the fit at five in the afternoon
one wonders if Bruckner
was ever happy.

bus

When I think back to my first years in Mexico, the old rundown heaps of that memorable Route 100 circulate more punctually than before. All of them, regardless of their stops, bore that same number and there were no Routes 1, 15, or 50. Seats were often in short supply and once the aisle was full, there were always people scattered among the seated passengers, standing with nothing to hold on to. Through the vanilla or coconut aromas of a basket of popular confections on their way to be sold in the streets, one would stumble into a sudden smell of henhouse: on the floor, an Otomi skirt concealed a bouquet of chickens bound at the feet. Sometimes a clandestine cigarette complexified odors you largely assumed would be bodily. It was to be expected. At 30 degrees centigrade in those ramshackle wrecks – exhaust from the engine could sometimes seep in through a broken section of floorboard – the journey across town was a harrowing experience: next time we should wait for a bus in better condition. But suffering the sun on a street corner among fumes from the dump trucks – those so-called *materialistas* – and the same buses whose interiors we were evading was equally atrocious and made us late. I refused to drive, terrified by the traffic, but at last I was forced to accept that not doing so meant belonging to a group of humans prone to annihilation and so I relented. I gained time and comfort. But I was slightly less free, I missed the litanies from the vendors of useless objects, the verbal inventions of a population with a particular gift for them, the reading I used to do during the trip, and ultimately a certain pleasant irresponsibility.

II

Under the watchful eye of the driver, they sit quietly, well-behaved, so as not to be cast out of Paradise. They know that only by placing their presumed freedom inside parentheses, will the established freedom tolerate them in its rolling bosom. Indeed, they know they have the right to bear every bodily smell imaginable and bring them aboard, to the chagrin of the other passengers, but the slightest vocal or gesticular unruliness, the kind that arise from an excess of alcohol, is enough for the Authority to make its way to the back after stopping the vehicle of course – and thus more vigilantly irritated – with no other sword but an ominous finger to point at the door in an inescapable gesture. I said the back because a custom undoubtedly driven by the discreet need to distance themselves from that black angel dictates that they choose this secession. And I say black because like in southern biblical stories the Almighty is oftentimes that 'supremely dark' color or reflects no visible radiation. They are usually those most zealous for order in their kingdom, those who never concede an unscheduled stop or unstipulated attention. I never saw anyone fight back. The censured descend, downcast and laggard, with a grumble at most and sometimes with assistance to prevent accidents given their state. A simple gesture has created two camps: one that continues on their journey and one that is now landbound, wherever, shrouded in solitude and fumes. But only for a few minutes until the next Austinite bus picks them up on a trial basis.

III

In another city, the descent can be contentious even when not mandatory. If someone accustomed to more general services and practices attempts to make use of that cord strung above the windows, believing it destined to inform the driver of their desire to exit, they will most likely trigger a reaction, a prophesy, a rebuke. Civil rights and labor laws will manifest in the mouth and gestures of an impolite – save for some exceptions – and uneconomic institution: the bus attendant. They are in charge of relaying the passenger's decision to the driver. This should be expressed in a high-pitched and unambiguous whistle that covers other possible noises, like the conversation between the two public servants or the usually deafening radio that at certain hours offers an exemplarily vulgar listening experience. The attendant and the driver are separated by little more than a meter and the audible signal reaches them both equally. If the descent is realized through the rear doors, then the attendant will fulfill their essential function: with another ring of the bell, they give the order to depart. A vestige of an era when they helped the elderly and pregnant women or women with children get on and off, and with courtesy now in decline – a symptom of classism – the attendant is a rarity prized by tourists. They usually express themselves in gerunds: *coming through, getting off.*

C

C

Driven by their juridic obsession, the Romans called it *littera tristis*. They remembered that judges once used it when voting to abbreviate their *condemno* and their severity, which they undoubtedly abused. While I am not certain of it, the Christians may have also joined in the scorn, finding it culpable of the disturbing crucifixion. I see it as a modest, timid letter that stopped short of becoming many others: *o*, *a*, *d*, *g*, *q*, content to calm, cure, chant, celebrate, perhaps not so much to charge, clone, cripple, censure, or castigate. From this, not even a letter can escape.

Cabrerita

I lived in Paris for a few months the only way possible: convinced that my stay had no time limit. I amused myself sometimes by getting off at a random subway station. Winter was approaching and I would suddenly emerge to a light that jostled for a place in the truncated afternoon. It was not entirely an adventure; it was conditioned by the prudence of a specific timetable and the desire to avoid an overly labyrinthine journey when the time came to return usually late and exhausted to the *Cité Universitaire*, my starting point. I considered myself a tireless walker. This expression, I believe, refers to those who walk more than others and joyfully, without excluding the joy we get from the rest at the end of the journey. At least this has always been my case, especially in Paris.

I improvised the discreet musical score of a housewife out shopping, more befitting my age than the night owl scholar I in fact was. That particular time I got off at Denfert-Rochereau. I walked down a polished cobblestone road lined with small shops waiting behind their doors closed to the cold, slightly regretful of my choice, when amid that color-lessness we accept as one of the flavors of Paris, I recognized a familiar patch of soft tones, pink, pale green, and yellow on a poster stuck to the inside of a store window. The window belonged to an unremarkable real estate company. The poster, on the other hand, was like the mouth of a pitcher filled with magical water, that water for which my thirst is always prepared. What was Cabrerita's unmistakable watercolor, pure clumsiness and lyricism, doing in that residential Parisian quarter? Raúl Javiel Cabrera, whom I continue to regard as the most essentially Montevidean of Montevidean painters of his time. The poster announced a reading at a theater I do not recall by his lifelong friend José Parrilla, poet and successful guru somewhere on the Côte d'Azur, I had heard. Actually, it was not him who was reading but a group of actors.

But Parrilla and his rambling lifestyle is another story, like a drawing with dotted strokes that someone might complete one day. His name there explained the serendipitous and almost magical appearance of a theme, a line, a color that were not of that place and time and yet leapt toward me with fragile simplicity from the drizzly foreign sunset. But logic insists on closely pursuing wonder, regardless of whether the explanation will disappoint us. Some would say we should be grateful for this disposition, necessary to add balance to our quotidian footsteps. Not all of us are allowed to pass behind the curtains that various distances hang and walk through ghostlands.

Though I did not know it in that moment, Cabrerita was still alive in Montevideo, which may have been his birthplace but was where he spent his earliest days of childhood until his death, save for a brief parenthesis: Parilla brought him to live in Europe for a time. The peculiar painter found the change unsettling. He was a poor and unassuming man and perhaps saw himself surrounded by a comfort he could not understand. An astute jury had once awarded him a minor prize at a National Gallery of Art. He used it to pay for a sensible overcoat someone convinced him to buy, for a steady stream of café con leche, and an unknown number of taxi rides, the only luxuries the painter desired. His mental state showed signs of being as precarious as his health. He spent several years in a psychiatric hospital. He met doctors who helped him, friends who supplied him with paper, brushes, watercolors. There were periods when he ate his erasers. During others, he continued to paint. A family cared for him for his final years in an environment that was more humane than Hospital Vilardebó.

He had disappeared from Montevideo's tight-knit cultural world well before his death at the end of 1992. I doubt today's youth know who he was, but if Figari's paintings could bring to life a past he was able to experience, with gaucho women and black communities and ranch courtyards and melancholic horses and ombú trees like an oasis of shade, then Cabrerita unwittingly represents, through his neglect, through those illusory little girls, the spaces without mystery in neighborhoods known to any Montevidean.

In 1947 or 48, I was entering a café downtown next to an Ateneo that was prestigious at the time. Poor and diminutive, Cabrerita – as he was always called – used to wander from one table to another peddling his watercolors. He only accepted café con leche and croissants as payment. But at that moment, standing in the doorway with an indecisive air about him, he was perhaps planning to use the public phone. Was that a normal activity for him? What I know for certain is that a coin suddenly appeared in his slightly open hand, placed there by a passerby. Cabrerita sold, he did not beg. When he looked up and saw that I had been an accidental witness to that scene, he explained it to me: 'A psychological dilemma has just arisen.' On more than one occasion, he approached a group I was in and dutifully extended his hand, a cold and slippery fish, to everyone there seated. But he did not make conversation.

The watercolors of his that we have were bought at an exhibition organized for him back then at the Ateneo. The prices were modest and affordable for even the humblest of patrons. I have never seen one of his works, a scribble dashed off by his hand, and not recognized it. I am not sure if that suffices to confirm his singularity, his value in that class of naïve moderns. I would say he was a natural painter, that without teachers he had learned for himself.

He gleamed with a particular admiration that he made no effort to keep secret. New acquaintances were appraised with a question: 'Have you heard of Jean Coteau?' The name, missing its second *c*, was pronounced in Spanish, heavily stressing the *a*. Was it the poet he admired or the artist?

I do not know if he painted with oils. Watercolor was his medium. Lewis Carroll photographed girls, Cabrerita painted them. Imaginary, alone, in groups, some peering through windows, others playing with hoops, running, with big eyes, blondes or brunettes, with bows in their hair or strange hairdos, but always small young women, protuberant and out of proportion, whose ruffled skirts tied with ribbons were often too short, revealing knees that were not at all childlike and legs with curvaceous calves. He drew them with strokes in sepia later covered with a choir of innocent colors, kitschy nainsook light greens, undergarment pinks. But he also painted portraits, at least when he was young. Or one portrait of Carlos Maggi, who had let him stay at his house for a few days (and whose mother had fed him just as he liked, with café con leche following a system that today they would call an open bar). The likeness left nothing to be desired.

While he typically used the paper itself as background (maybe due to the limited materials available to him), one of the watercolors in my possession is heavily laden with color and every inch of it painted: a woman's head in profile occupies most of the space; half of another facing forward peeks out to the side. The first encloses more heads, as if imagining them: it has been invaded by the vision of those obsessive girls who fill the streets with their enigmatic games. The white radiating daylight, his

31

usual illumination, covered with overlapping reds and greens, that is, with oppressive purples, suggests a change in mood where only the fixations and brush-strokes remind us of the artist.

There were no girls in the other painting I chose, although its parentage was undeniable. Chestnut-colored profiles filtering through a stationary green, the figures were unusual compared to all the other paintings on exhibit: two knights, symmetrical, each holding a shield and leaning to one side of their mounts, which were two halves of two horses facing one another from opposite borders of the page, not quite the edges, where he had scrupulously drawn the line that fractured them.

But apart from these two works, I am not aware of other instances in which those primordial girls, alone or gathered together, were not the primary, if not only, theme. I am not saying none exist, but I have not seen them. A showcase of his later works might reveal other forms in his loyalty to painting with which he overcame the circumstances of a sad and tormented life.

But I have not yet finished the story of the poster. It effectively called attention to the reading at the theater but without belying its provenance: there was no date, making it impossible to know if the event was happening, going to happen, or if it had already become a part of urban microhistory. I entered the shop – bells ringing loudly – to ask how long the announcement had been there. The man who assisted me seemed to realize in that instant what he was displaying in his shop window and had it expeditiously removed and given to me. A minute later I was back in the street, poster in hand, but with no information regarding its expiration.

My excitement did not prevent me from entering a nearby shoe store and buying a much-needed pair for the rain. When I got back to the warmth of my room, ate, and left breakfast for the tits,[2] I noticed I no longer had my rolled-up Cabrerita. The next morning, I re-enacted my journey to retrieve it from the shoe seller's backroom, who took it down with sadness, she told me, because she had liked it very much.

calligraphy

At what age does one's aesthetic curiosity awaken? I do not equate the choice a human animal makes in the first months of its life between one color and another with the one it might make decades later between Nolde and Dix. And of course no two experiences are the same. As a child I liked everything, conventionally so but with certain baroque tendencies. Or many things: the diminutive Solomonic columns of the Atwater Kent (a splendid primitive radio that granted me shortwave access with the simple flip of a switch, something that was impossible in later models); the artificial bouquet of holly (mother-of-pearl leaves and red berries); the thick embossed wallpaper in muted hues of green, purple, and brown (I treasured a leftover scrap as if it were a talisman and for years it protected my Royal Spanish Academy Dictionary); the alabaster centerpiece (trays ascending from large to small with tiny birds about the edges, relocated to the sideboard); the red Murano glassware in the china cabinet. These examples are from the dining room, perhaps because eating bored me, and

---

[2] Small birds common throughout Europe, considered to be very intelligent, ravenous for butter during hard times.

I spent the time generated by my persistent procrastination looking not at the impatient adults but at these indifferent objects. Without knowing why, I preferred certain things, certain forms, certain sheens, colors, and transparencies to the restrained opacity of everything else (humans included).

I first participated in an aesthetic project, fully aware now of what was happening, when I began copying pages of calligraphy. It was good to have a model, even if it seemed unattainable, and to compare my latest efforts with previous ones. My life's earliest conscious artistic devotions were the various curves that English cursive requires for the elegant flourishes of its capital letters, the G, L, or S, almost all of them really, the exact point of tangency between the X's two semicircles, the need for the F's upper stroke and the lower bar that fractures its stem to be harmoniously parallel.

We start to draw before we write; drawing is spontaneous, almost as natural as speaking. Whenever paper and pencil are within a child's reach, they will draw. Some genius drew on stones. But until adult intervention arrives, Divine Arbitrariness is its only guide. Calligraphy has laws.

If the reader was not startled by my mention of calligraphy, that denigrated subject lying in the ashes of modernity's many fires, then you belong to a lost generation, by which I mean that, like me, you are beginning to disappear into the mists of time. (Have you noticed that the technological advances with which the twentieth century sought to consecrate itself are hurtling you through a twenty-first century that welcomes you like an intruder?) For many lustrums now, the teaching of this highly useful art has been disregarded in the greater (or worser) part of the world. There is no use lauding it at this point. All the same, I will.

1) It is a manual art and, as such, it promotes dexterity in precision and subtlety. It is well known that discipline of the hands resonates in the brain and assists in its development. Or does all this pedagogical to-do intend for people to limit themselves to watching a television or moving a mouse?

2) It demands order. A positive result cannot be achieved without following, one by one, certain previous movements.

3) It accustoms us to quietude. It does not admit haste or nerves. It is intimately associated with a time that is, we might say, out-of-time, like any artisanal craft, with a time that merges with space, as Jung liked to say when talking about those coordinates of bodies in motion.

4) And to meticulousness. A clean, unwrinkled page; an exemplary pen, obedient and free of lint; and equally deserving hands are essential.

5) It teaches the necessary admiration for the good handiwork of others.[3]

---

[3]   If I do not include a personal experience here, when will I? The opportunity in life to talk about such a subject is as doubtful as finding a quill in a haystack. Continuing a family tradition of good penmanship and jaunty signatures, I was best in my class at calligraphy, but not in mathematics, proof positive that I always preferred what was destined for disaster. Apart from the honor, this presented me with certain complications. My teacher, dear, kind Pía Cúneo handled this with encouraging and very personal corrections. Her handwriting, which I would recognize among a hundred others, fell discreetly behind the canon; for that reason, during my sixth-grade year, group A, I was charged with the labels that graced the covers of our notebooks and that, due to some unknown tradition, were written by the teachers. For the first time, I had to perform a community service, a task that was dark, secret (or almost), and exhausting

6) And in the long run, the necessary independence to deviate from the norm, once well learned, and develop our own design, which is one of personality's contours. (How can I not mention 'contours', one of the things we abandon when this moment – adulthood – arrives, along with our special pen, be it a Perry or a Lincoln?)[4]

---

since each student used several notebooks and there were more than thirty of us. Violeta Aldabe was short, chubby, and sweet and had the worst handwriting in the class. I suspect Pía was relentless with that extreme case. I have no idea how she sensed the self-love hidden behind the girl's timid script. Holy Week and its vacation arrived, and Violeta headed into it armed with practice pages. Seven days later, she displayed her spectacular results in notebooks and on the chalkboard. Her handwriting was nothing like it was before. Nor was it like that of our teacher, who had now been surpassed by two of her students. I had great respect for that triumphant effort, knowing that my calligraphic virtues – which I let last only a short time – were merely the result of habit and had it been otherwise, she would have perhaps been incapable of such a dramatic change.

Once that and the rest of my school years had ended, I never again heard any news of Violeta, but I think of her every time I picture Juan Ramón Jiménez engaged in the inverse task of abandoning the norm, during a time period that perhaps some biographer has determined, erasing the burden of widespread English cursive to devote himself to inventing, coherent with his poetry, a thing of beauty that spoke Spanish with an almost uninterrupted Arabic graphism. Discovering his beautiful design – I still have a sample of it that is almost entirely foxed with freckles – many years after those practice sheets, enlightened me on the need to unlearn what is dutifully learned, while also showing me that it is best to toss aside the rind of the substance that has already nourished us. This circular gesture reintegrates our nature with the joyful possibility of creation, whatever it may be.

[4] As I revise this text, I remember *Encyclopedia of a Life in Russia*, 'organized into entries or voices', by my friend José Manuel Prieto, who under this same voice says: 'Her calligraphic writing revealed the ease with which she moved inside a universe of clockwork precision,

caprice

One did not always get it right. How remote some tastes from my early adolescence feel to me today. It was delusion more than taste that led me to Rimsky-Korsakov's *Capriccio Espagnol*, performed by the Monte Carlo Ballet and filmed on their home stage. I spent the little monthly allowance I was given to see it six times in one week at a movie theater that screened continuous showings. This system existed to bring you newsreels, trips to picturesque destinations, cartoons, and cultural short films. Expertly familiarizing myself with the programming order, I went to the theater three times, always walking in just before the object of my devotion was set to start. Tolerating all the rest and offering my impatience in sacrifice, I attended those golden minutes for a second time. The set design and dancing were accompanied by music I found fascinating. The night's blue backdrop, the red dresses, the black velvet invigorated by the new world of Technicolor were accompanied by the meaty density of that hybrid of Majorcan boleros stewed in the Russian composer's lavish orchestration, and everything was dazzling. Through this exciting initiation, I learned the practice of a form of idolatry that I would apply more accurately in the future.

---

blindly guided by discipline. That was the cause of her unwavering good humor. I would never be able to achieve such handwriting. L★, however, was upstanding and possessed all the grace of the flourishes on her capital letters…

"You know what? I always thought calligraphy was a thing of the past, from the days when my father studied it using the Edward Johnston system and beautiful Packards scrolled through the streets, which were like calligraphy compared to the names of today's cars, written in block letters.'" I am happy that he too has seen the bond between canonical writing and the beautiful unexplored qualities of the spirit.

The spell of something that evaporated so quickly before me raised a barrier to the world. This world was the assemblage of couples, uninterested in that sea of colors and those rhythms I found mind-blowing, who had come searching for a bubble of relative intimacy in which to isolate themselves. Or it was those fluorescent eyes that cast their fishing, prehensile gazes from the shadows. Sometimes the casters stealthily advanced towards a seat slightly closer to me. An audible snarl was enough to be left in peace. These were lessons in silence: they were startled by the noise that repelled and denounced them and by the danger that the usher might come to remove them from their hiding place and larval state. Adept at this common custom, they could recognize on the fly what was and was not possible. A failure for one was a failure for all. Consequently, it was enough to ruffle the waters once for no one else to disturb me in my solitary worship. Today, free to imagine that the rest of the spectators were there by accident, I wonder how many of them still retain memories of that integral *Capriccio*.

I never heard of it being shown again, not even on television, and my suspicions regarding its possible sensationalism went unconfirmed. The music fell out of my list of favorites decades ago. However, it sometimes comes on the radio and, before switching it off, I picture for a second a vague hem, red, blue, and black, flung in the air to a rhythm that breaks and varies and refuses to go away no matter how much I wish it would.

cardinal

A blue cardinal warbles, color blind, at a crossroads of wings and cardoons.

caryopsis

of the oat,
samara of the elm,
samara of the ailanthus,
paired samara of the sycamore maple,
achene of the buckwheat,
follicle of the larkspur,
legume of the pea plant,
silicle of the wallflower,
silicle of the shepherd's purse,
capsule of the poppy,
balaustine of the pomegranate,
fruit of the blackberry bush,
segmented hesperidium of the orange tree,
berry of the belladonna.

Word-fruits
of the juicy life of language.

cemetery

I

In my memory I saw Cemetery Hill[5] appear in the
shape of Cerro Batoví ('Breast of a Virgin'), along
with assumptions of cheerful indigenes, in a state of
nature and good-natured, just as anyone well trained
during the eighteenth century might have envisioned
them. But with me the test did not bear its intended
fruit because the shape was more suggestive of a
hat fallen to the ground. When seen up-close, its
wide brim, an impeccable, Van Goghian pale green,
decomposes into multiple tiny yellow flowers over
an intense green. But the crown transforms into an

---

[5]   Tacuarembó, Uruguay.

unexpected embassy of terror: the wall is riddled with niches, gaping maws consuming crumbling wooden boxes, canisters spilling forth the bones of children and younger or older adults, depending on the case. It seems that since the time of the European Middle Ages – which this land knew nothing of – a macabre dance has been rattling ossuaries, raising lids, opening mandibles more or less intact, using femurs to beat on spectral drums and, once tired, tossing them far from their place. Père Lachaise, one of the deadest cemeteries I have seen, surrendered its inhabitants to nature, who destroys them by enveloping the tombs, gutting them, sinking its green fingernails and long woody arms into them, bursting bronze bolts, amphoras, and lachrymatories, fracturing marble slabs as if they were cookies fresh from the oven. This unstoppable domination coats misery in an imploring green moss that softens everything with its patina. And then there is the glory of the names. Discovering Musset's tomb, sullen and worn, where the will of various generations has not managed to get the sad willow he requested to take root, has its own melancholic zest. There is no resemblance between that theatrical death, where ruin is an aesthetic factor that piques the mystery, and the incurable despair of this hill with its poverty exposed to the sun and rain, to the wind and inclement footsteps of men without prejudice. Here the dead were abandoned with no attempt to withdraw them into that reclaiming breast. The precarious containers are quickly destroyed and their contents returned to the earth in the solitude of the countryside. There are small decaying Virgin Marys, ancient dates devoured by rust. We are transported to the middle of the last century, but such a leap backwards is not enough to explain this incredible cemetery. Our usual psychology, which seeks out roofs and refuge, could not have chosen this elevation bared to the winds, without a tree to offer its shade or the affective shelter that man, so confident in everything, has nevertheless become accustomed to demanding of it. No doubt, this isolated and miserable columbarium, without pigeons or columns and most of all without foliage, should be accepted as a distant legacy.

II

The Muzhik runs spiraling up the hill and when he reaches us, he announces he has come to claim an inheritance. Next to a half-open urn inside a niche the bees are buzzing, unaware of the abysmal classical contradiction they present, the frenzy of metaphors they propose. The Muzhik declares his intent without apprehension: 'They are making honey inside my uncle's skull. That honey belongs to me.' Though he has not found any nuncupative document or clause whatsoever, he is eager to possess the harvest, undeterred by the inconvenience of any sort of lugubrious affiliation. He kindly invites us to participate in the task, but nobody is particularly enraptured by that possibility. There he stays, left behind. As we descend the slope, navigating the crosses lying over the last of the tombs, the slightly bitter light of the sunset might very well be sustained, back there, by the smoke of his apiarian activities.

chance

An unexpected loving embrace in an air we sense to be veracious, a clarity that is the means and the end, dual. I discovered its existence and propositions when I was an adolescent who devoured everything, knowledgeable of her ignorance. From one text to the next, I saw the formation of relationships that were not nearly as strange as the fact they had been made visible to me at that precise moment. By this I mean I was drawn to reading books that, though chosen at random, turned out to be serialized by the common appearance of some subject or name that began to obsess me. I entered a vortex where what was exceedingly vertiginous was that everything remained still and I was the one whirled about bearing witness to a secret alliance. To this day I can remember an inexplicable happiness, an irrefutable state of confirmation – but of what? – triggered by my doubt concerning a verse, 'procuratorial wind of mirrors', written as I listened to something from Bach, and my discovery that I had been listening to one of his two 'mirrored' fugues from *The Art of Fugue*.

One time it is the unexpected encounter with someone I was just thinking about. Another time, a joke about *langue et parole* reminds us of Nora Parola, a student of Enrique who for years has been living in Paris. We remember her fondly but unbeknown to us, she is in Montevideo and minutes later we receive her phone call, leaving us speechless. Other times other conjunctions occur. An example:'*carpetovetónico*' is used in Spain to refer to a central mountain range and, by extension, to a Spaniard whose mindset is very traditional, obtuse. Spanish dictionaries used to be very traditional; at least those I consulted did not register this word. I had been able to live without it until one month in 1982, I think, when I came across it in an old book by Cintio Vitier. We were living in Mexico. Two days later it appeared in an article by José de la Colina. A week later, as I enunciated each of its syllables, chewing on it, lugging it around with me on my every outing to see if I might locate its parents only to be met with silence by the majority of those asked – I have no idea why I had not called Pepe (yes, I do: I wanted a spectacular revelation) – it re-emerged, strangely, in the translation of an interview with Robbe-Grillet. That gadfly and its derisive buzzing would still have time to show up once more before África and Jorge Villegas, charming Spanish friends facing my now routine question, explained with a certain amount of outrage that this was something taught in schools. I defended myself: not in mine, so far away and maritime. The important thing was that with my lexicon now enriched, nothing was ever again serially Carpetovetonic. The circle had been closed.

We do not always simply graze a hornet's nest. Sometimes we suffer a head-on collision. One night we went to the cinema to see a classic film, *Lola* by Jacques Demy, dedicated to Max Ophüls and his own *Lola*. On our way back we commented on its parodic tone, the Molièresque rhythm of the encounters and, especially, the misencounters between Lola, a dancer in a small cabaret, and her beloved sailor – the father of her son – for whom she has been faithfully waiting for seven years. The entire film builds towards him finding Lola, having returned a rich man. At home and before going to bed, the images give way to pages. I pick up a book at random. Per Olov Enquist writes that he wanted to undertake a bildungsroman. On the verge of losing interest (I had never read anything of his), a line in italics catches my eye: *Le tournant s'est fait lorsque j'ai vu* Lola *de Jacques Demy.*[6]

---

[6]   The change occurred when I saw *Lola* by Jacques Demy.

This is followed by a long passage about the film. No, I do not rub my eyes in disbelief, I open them wide and demand Enrique's attention, my only witness. The night before, I had walked among the shelves of the enormous library – six extensive floors – at the university. On a bottom shelf I discovered several volumes of *Les lettres nouvelles*. Seated on the carpet, I confirmed the title's provisionality: they are from the seventies and part of the material is no longer new. But for many years I have been under the sinister spell of Stig Dagerman and in the issue dedicated to Finland and Sweden there is one of his short stories. So, in November of 1991 I picked out a journal published in February of 1972, which I will be the first to read (a pristine checkout card confirms this). The next night I would turn not to Dagerman but to the unknown Enquist, who in 1966 had referred to what was for him a decisive *Lola*, which I would see twenty-five years later when everything would coincide here, in a point in space called Austin. Per Olov Enquist's text begins: 'Every writer is the result of a series of chance occurrences.'

I cannot resist the temptation of one last example, maybe because as long as they continue to happen, I continue to feel alive. I am writing an article for a collective issue on Montevideo. My Montevideo is entirely internal and largely phantasmal. Certain that very few people will have any interest in reading it, I have decided to talk about its image in the works of travel writers such as Hofmannsthal, among others. During one of his trips, he docked in Montevideo. In a brief text, he tells of a young Englishman lying in a neighboring hospital bed where the Austrian writer was forced to seek treatment and of a phrase spoken by the former, who had heard it from his father. It went something like: 'Man should give of himself entirely once and for all.' That phrase seemed to me to have some relation to other opacities, but from where and from whom? I prepared myself for a long period of curiosity since it had taken me almost thirty years of useless trawling to discover that those mysterious *Utopians from Salento* came from Fénelon...

The young Englishman's little phrase had distracted me. When one gets stuck, nothing better than a cup of tea. And there is nothing better to accompany those minutes of tea, if not another human being, than a book chosen at random. Returning, cup in hand, down a long corridor of books, I doubted for an instant and then grabbed Lichtenberg's aphorisms, which I had not read in a good while and whose virginity is restored now and again thanks to my bad memory. Hardly had I leafed through it when there it was, the phrase, which turned out to be a quotation from Addison. Perhaps Hofmannsthal had found it in the same place. I drank my cup of tea with religious exhilaration, in honor of Chance, praying that its assistance would never forsake me, at least not until that moment we assume is not coincidental, but inevitable.

chaos

With little originality, I imagine chaos to be a formless, infinite, enraged mass, a vast mound of excesses, ones inserted inside others, an even more confusing amphisbaena, the contrary of the Tao. I am no doubt informed by the Greek Chaos and by the idea of what holds up those waters over which hovers the spirit of God, the Vulgate's *inane* and *vacuo*, the Hebrew *tohu wa-bohu*, which includes the ideas of desert and nothingness. And I also add to it, no doubt, the transformation it was given by the French language, *tohu-bohu*, an accumulation of confusion and noise.

But could it not be a smooth space, obscuring and bounded, a merciless order whose meaning escapes us? Chaos does not need grand magnitude of spirit to subjugate everything to its nature, nor much time for its disquieting effect. We are not among those few who administer Truth in a strategy of domination that is renewed every now and then. Everything is chaos because they exist. Beauty, love are suddenly struck by chaos, the line spanning from birth to death becomes entangled and is chaos. And what of that brief moment when the fragrant privet blooms, superimposing itself over disconcertion and ugliness? Is it too the visible manifestation of chaos or is it the tiny fissure through which a slow emergence begins, one that could give rise to a new concert, a serenity of calm and voluntary acts, the return of grace?

chess

The absurd struggle burns across the board,
the pawns advance
their feeble agonizing game
or resort to deceitful repose.
The tower totters, hastens
destiny, disaster,
the knights yield following
a toppling twist of bishops.
The king is no more.

Only the queen,
mistress of useless powers,
prolongs the futile nightmare,
creating and destroying blind diagonals,
losing her clean death.

chimera

At least I am not alone when it comes to being made up of odds and ends, disparate elements, foolproof; there are many other creatures, ones I do not care to remember – in my Greek world alone: cerberuses, centaurs, gorgons, harpies, sirens... But perhaps such a farrago only fell to me. A variety of sources, they might say. If the goal is a terrifying outcome, then placing a lion's head at its fore-end assures success; finishing it as a serpent – some say a dragon – adds its own special touch. But I would have asked for more imagination, less measured symmetry of opposites. The two extremes decided, whoever was charged with imagining me seemingly let their guard down when they reached my core. Linking lion and snake or dragon by way of goat decreases efficacy in what, as I already admitted, was not bad. A goat... As a matter of body, it is not the most prestigious.

An anatomy conceived to leap and bound? Why not? But if that was their intention, and that my leaps and bounds be swift – a myth cannot stagger along – then they should have correctly calculated the weights and complied with certain demands of proportion. I would have those responsible put to the test. I once tried, and it was one of my defeats. One head weighs heavy. But what about two? Because whether it was to avoid waste or a legacy from my mother the Hydra, who knew how to manage with seven, they also gave me the head of a goat. Those who have tried to draw me or sculpt me bang their own against walls trying to insert one and then another. My mother's heads – how well I remember her – were all of the same model and therefore harmonious and able to aim in the same direction when she breathed fire with identical and precise fury, not without pretense. At least they afforded me the recourse of her igneous fits of rage.

As for the rest of me, what can I do with this structural atrocity that nobody entirely understands? Some confuse me with Medusa, in some places they conflate me with the hircocervus. In both cases I come off favorably in comparison, but we are who we are and do not change on the way and *à chaque fou plait sa marotte*.[7] Bellerophon succeeded in slaying me thanks to Pegasus, another compound being but with moderation: an eagle's wings sit well on a horse, and someone must have said: 'Don't touch it any more!' My defeat proved that additional elements do not lead to greater efficacy. Nor beauty, alas. But men misconstrue everything. Rather than come to this conclusion and forget about me, little by little they have elevated me, almost godlike, to the realm of their most glorious and impossible dreams. There I now achieve my supreme perfection. Fire, heads, ungracious body, tail: nothing matters, all is reconciled. The odds and ends have been forgotten, the ugliness corrected, and when they are captivated by something too beautiful and remote that compels them forward, impossible to ever reach, they evoke my name and sigh. Who thinks then of Bellerophon, of Pegasus?

circle

The circle is a figure with the potential to be expansive, comprehensive, and kind. The vicious circle is a minor subspecies, violent and closed, that orbits in melancholic discussions.

---

[7] Every fool likes their own bauble best.

clock

> The musicalizing froze
> just as the clock strikes one,
> with ox-like toleration
> to the other side it goes.
>
> Alone, the spirit bewails,
> when the bell rings out at two,
> that time has flown by while you
> were bound by routine travails.
>
> The tasks in the kitchen intoned
> – as soon as it's two it's three –
> again, and insipidly,
> what matters most is postponed.
>
> Patience at last starts to flower
> between four o'clock or five.
> The soul, which has sprung to life,
> was able to forget the hour.
>
> And this will persist, if blessed,
> from six o'clock until twelve.
> Then you lose the joy to live
> and instead rehearse for death.

codo

> Why does the English 'elbow' sound like a bell or a
> flower while this lamentable word of ours has not so
> much as a petal?

color

> Nothing easier, nothing more difficult than making

it to the factory of colors, an age-old factory. When going in search of it, you must set out in the twilight at dawn or dusk walking in a straight line, in any direction, without stopping or veering off course until the following twilight. On that spot you will find the tree that Pierre de Beauvais named the Peridexion, meaning 'on the right side'. You must not be distracted by the doves asleep in its branches, cooing melodiously even while sleeping, or by the dragon that feeds on them without their numbers ever decreasing. You will have to take nine long strides forward with your eyes closed and open them slowly to avoid being blinded. There we will find it, splendid.

There red transforms into ripened pepper, rose, hummingbird fuchsia, crab leg and the shell of the maja squinado, terracotta, Little Red Riding Hood's little hood, fez, an extravagant woman's fingernail, devil, ruby, flame, kapok or poinciana flower, carnelian, coral, blood; orange… oranges, egg yolk, and Mexican marigold. Black comes out as hair, ink, soot, as jet and black cat and dark horse and canary eye and moonless night. Blue comes out in small portions and becomes sky and baby blue eyes and sapphire and aquamarine and water of the high seas and forget-me-nots and other small flowers, which blossom in countrysides without us knowing their almost secret names. Green… so much green is needed, given the high demand from grasses, foliage for trees, flower stems, mantises, *mamboretás*, lizards. It also ends up in cat's eyes and human eyes, in emeralds and parrots. The most dangerous green determines certain poisons, little innocent-looking frogs, develops in hidden mosses, thrives in vegetal velvets that disguise swamps where strayed animals sink, distractions are punished, and vengeances are wreaked. Violet is used to color eyes that only appear in literature, but violets and amethysts take up almost all of it, with soft remnants dissolving in daily sunsets and distant mountains, faraway places, first shadows.

No excess color is wasted. Bits of blue and yellow make the glaucous shade for the pristine waters in certain caverns, for certain gazes. Everything is darkened with scraps of black, also used with dabs of red, yellow, and white in stones, animal skins, tree trunks. If we only add white to the black, we get the gray in our grandfather's and grandmother's hair, storm clouds, bagworm cocoons.

On occasion, the pigments get momentarily jammed, but the work does not stop. So much white then for snow, clouds, eggshells, foams, innocence and lustrous white hair, rabbits, swans and petals on daisies, jasmines, and magnolias, every white flower in the world and every wedding dress. There is no shortage of hue fanatics who seek countless varieties for countless things, which we invented dictionaries to manage but they will never succeed in defining the totality of gradations, one of creation's least regarded treasures.

Concepción[8]

Since she forgot to fill her lamp with oil
for the weddings of the prestigious,
she has been left shining in the shadows
while everyone else's swift carriages go by.

---

[8]   Concepción Silva Belinzón.

creature

Chrysalis of stature, which a scream (*cri*) erases (*rature*).
Chrysalis on a hiatus, weary of stature.

cricket

In the clarity of night
the cricket, not man, sings
in any garden
where paradise appears.
Coarse sonorous salt
and also sweet jasmine
that grows and creates the swaying horizon;
it is the star and its echo,
silence and clamorous canticle,
secret concurrence
where all limits coincide.

crossroads

How can we be sure that an avenue, boulevard,
or simple road is not a blind alley? The inevitable
trees that line them, poplars or not, may lead farther
ahead to a narrowing, a bleakness, a quagmire,
while expansion can reach the extraversion of all
boundaries.

And take care not to forget the risk posed by
a crossroads. There all peace comes to an end.
Nostalgia might, perhaps, begin. Or, per mishaps,
anxiety, conflict, and urgency. In early times, a choice
implied the intervention of destiny, always unpredictable, mysterious, and fraught with risks. The
Romans sent minor deities to all corners to fulfill
particular functions; for the vigilance and protection
of the perilous crossroads, they imagined the Lares

Compitales and celebrated the Compitalia to gain their favor.

Nowadays, the anxiety felt at the danger of a demon, ghost, or troll that folklore summoned to the air of a crossroads (Cunqueiro would herald a dwarf) is often substituted by the anxiety of having to make a choice. Does not every intersection contain a circle, minute but a circle just the same and thus a magical mandala? There chance may be waiting, which for many is destiny (the first of the five 'logics of inertia' invented by Plutarch).

A country devoted for so long to the desolate gods of positivism and the firm distrust or prevention of any glimmer prone to manifestations of a divine power can be easy prey for Exu, the fallen angel. This name will not be as familiar to everyone as Satan or Lucifer, or simply the Devil, but by virtue of being several centuries younger in our world, he has gained followers of modern forms of religious speculation, like the magic of Quimbanda, which is apparently inclined towards evil. In contrast, Umbanda is wielded for good…

Exu reigns in the former under the many names to which he must answer. Among them Exu Tiriri has the nicest ring to it, though one would do best not to trust his tintinnabulation since Exu Tiriri, who also watches over the crossroads, is malevolent and mischievous like a British trilby. Slightly more exhibitionist, according to those who know about these things, he takes pleasure in signaling his presence with a red light on his head, despite covering himself with a nebulous veil. Once again, the apprehension that a junction of roads has caused in every era, in every mythology, is confirmed. Besides the doubts they present, we risk the appearance of a demon under whichever name it fancies at that moment. This, however, is not a phenomenon anticipated by today's system of roadways.

When winding through the rolling countryside, some unassuming road will at some point face the incursion of another. Maybe someone, an inhabitant of an almost obsolete oral past, will be awaited there by a twisted ghost, more malevolent than ever: concentrated from disuse, he must despise the circulating world that ignores him and from an ordinary, low-ranking threat, he will become the increasingly powerful Exu Tiriri, devil of bells.

Cities have ultimately defeated the crossroads. Once a place of ambush, then disguised as a simple street corner, they want it to be harmless and have made it horrendous. They erect inhabited concrete masses, fatally exact, that vanquish the invisible silhouettes in the air. Irretrievably lost, mystery dissipates to the benefit of no one, like so many other things of the past. There is nowhere left in the world's organization to doubt and place yourself in destiny's hands.

But when we enter the arcane realm of the nightmare, it is easy for a crossroads to appear, a frequently used resource by its tireless office that is capable of conjuring them up even inside a wardrobe. We are saved upon waking, spared having to choose between options that will always be cruel.

custom

I

Custom, consumption of days,
ruin of wonders

eroding spume and plume.
What remains
is the dreadful framework,
disruption, discouragement,
a shaking of the cage
and inside
we divvy up the emptiness.

II

The spell is forever brief
or else it is custom, lifeless cetacean
injecting stupor into the most radiant beach
and rotting even the distant miracle.

D

danger

There were bonfires everywhere. They put them out one by one, at first distracted, now exhausted. It was useless. Others erupted behind them. The pistil of a flower started to wither and fell from its plant, immediately catching fire, a small brittle ember leaving its tiny scar on the polished wood floors. The day when an absentminded hand wrung notes from the piano, the flames rose dense like a geyser and descended with the scent of forest fire. They inhaled and were elevated to a sacramental and distant air. Sometimes the fire began without them knowing how. It was betrayed by a swarm of cinders floating past their heads, from East to West, coming from the bedroom toward the closed living room window. The one nearest to it swam momentarily submerged through that great density, opened a shutter, and returned with their eyes blackened. When there were visitors, a certain calm occurred. At most, a furtive crackle, like trampled matches, a high-pitched flickering, on and off, like fireflies in the nighttime meadows of summer. But between pauses the danger

weighed heavier and heavier and one day, with a
hushed and shared fear of ashes, they broached the
subject, treading lightly.

Darío

Unicorn of gold
word
dagger on hip
venerable nightingale
Clavileño breed
sphinx sword
eternal womb
visionary panic.

But also:
crash of crystals
infernal thorn
erratic cadaver
horror
the how
the when
melancholy.

And even:
limits of the wind
canopy of sorrows
ambiguous father
embittered yellow mask
sea of the people.

days

White days welcome precaution, swaddling it,
pouring over it, cinnamon over a flavorless dish, the

powdery residue of black days.

Black days rise iridescent in a reflection of planetary death.

White days are immune to the lugubrious bugling of bones, but they overwhelm hope by excessively demanding it practice cat pose and caressing it.

Black days have sinister executioner courtesies and academic rebukes.

White days are forgotten like praise for the uninspiring.

death

I

> *O Mort, très rabice bice*
> *Tu n'es pas genice nice*
> *Mais de doeul nourrice rice.*
> Jean Moulinet

We are all equal in death, said Manrique in times past with his medieval and theological eye on the moral plane. To differentiate ourselves is, then, to oppose death. Life is a process of separation. Hence Nietzsche's vital proposal: 'my morality would consist of gradually ridding man of his common traits, making him more specialized until he is incomprehensible to others.' Nevertheless, this century, like those prior, continues to work in Death's favor as if willing to do most of his work for him by providing an education that simplifies everything and tends to forget what truly matters. This means causing peculiarities to disappear or at least rendering them dull to the uninterested eye of others. Death, rejected on some planes, subtly filters into others: they inform us so as to uniform us, so that we think alike; they entertain us primarily with banalities, they dispute our every difference, even what we ourselves once were in a past they threaten us with like an imperative model. They prepare us for the Great Convergence. Marguerite Yourcenar suffered this ambush: *Je ne crois pas comme ils croient, je ne vis pas comme ils vivent, je n'aime pas comme ils aiment... Je mourrais comme ils meurent.*[9]

II

Death was first a small fugitive parrot crashing against a mantlepiece and falling into a pot of boiling water. Quickly inhumed, steeped green, shrouded in steam. After that, amongst the almost dendritic bunches of molds and cobwebs, the trunk with the cantankerous lid where Grandfather's things were kept secret, even more Masonic; and Aunt Ida's cambrics from his final night and the pink silk onto which fell the bitter denial of mourning. Last clothing that undoubtedly held miasmas without fulgurations, blunt memories of agonies and passings, refractory infinities yet contaminators of sadness, at least. Next would come the dying tear escaping the eye of the departed, in mysterious but undeniable agreement with his beard, black and fluffy like a suicide forest, which continued to grow, after hours, like the uninvited guest who arrives at the party once their only connection has left. And, seeing that, the young widow's terrified shriek, gasping at the incongruity. Later would come the long succession, penultimate for now, always depriving us of something, raptorial bull, never to return.

---

[9] 'I don't believe as they do, I don't live as they do, I don't love as they do... I will die as they die.'

deceased

In his *Dicionário Escolar do Português do Brasil* (updated by Osmar Barbosa), whose use is no less recommended despite being in a different but neighboring language, Don Antenor Nascentes offers a remarkable definition for 'deceased': *pessoa que já se desobrigou do encargo da vida. Encargo*: 'onerous state, obligation stemming from a task'. *Desobrigar*: 'to be released, to cease to be obligated, recognized, forced'. In other words, 'a person who has been released from the duty of life'. Compared to this elegance, how dull and insipid is the indifference of Casares's *Diccionario* (which has currently taken the place of the one that radiates elegance): 'a person who has died'. Its synonymous entry does nothing to redeem it: 'dead, no longer living'. Very bland. In contrast, a definition as encouraging, we might say as persuasive, as Don Antenor's almost compels us to aspire to that situation of the deceased, well rested and free of responsibilities. But is this leaving of everything, this definitive abandonment of the infinite ways of *being*, a situation or a state? I should learn from Mr. Nascentes and limit myself to the particular field in which I will not drivel on. Now as I mention him again, I am overjoyed to realize the generous spirit with which his surname takes on the category diametrically opposed to 'deceased'. This could be the reason why his work exhibits, perhaps more than that of any of his colleagues (I have only consulted Cândido de Figueiredo), such a refined attitude toward the metaphysical antipode of your author.

depression

The arc of our days, slack, sinks like a forsaken motive.

disconformity

Hearing him enumerate the number of anticipated precipices across the roads of the world, the cold waters he would encounter in the deep unavoidable channels, and the flaming tongues of the monsters that could accost him, she decided to break with her fascination for traveling and divide herself into impersonal pieces: as such, each one of them was more capable than the whole of devoting itself to the construction of bridges, parachutes, and quilts. At the same time, she imagined fashioning Altamiras and Lascauxs, anti-aircraft and anti-human shelters, cottonous coverings, and also accumulating small and easily distributed docility. He must have overcome his own disquiet some time later when she saw him checking the price of Dramamine and other preventatives against vertigo while casting nostalgic gazes over the towers and hustle and bustle of the airport. When they again spoke of dangers and explorations, velocities and whirrings, she realized there would never be any respite or escape possible from these repetitive cycles.

disjunction

A staff shall blossom or become a straw to grasp at.

division

The most complex of the basic operations a child will face. And the most terrible notion that will

accompany man his entire life, fractioning him with
each inescapable choice until he reaches death's
definitive partition.

dream

I

In the dream there were birds
birds forever burning,
allegories no doubt
and a magnificent garden,
pepper trees ferns casuarinas
countering the glacial certainty:

she'll walk across bridges,
she'll sit on fences,
smiling at ever unfamiliar stones,
she'll head into summer
like into a meadow of nettles
with no garden except the night's.

II

The mane slips from her hands
she flows into the plain she's alone
as fading confidence dissolves
the torrential horse at last smoke
that bore her through the wind
to the very edge of the precipice
to this anxious platform. It is day.
In dreams dilemmas are reborn.

ductility

The water shimmers over the fish, smells fetid over
its cadaver.

E

ecological

No, there will be no gardens. Nothing, only drought and desperation, stalks of straw trembling in the wind, and with this, the tragic carphologies that once announced an impending dark day and are perhaps now the only funeral rites for an annihilated world, gusts of pestilence mediating in solitude among cadavers. Sporadic roars perhaps still rasp some solitary corners of the earth. Will there be beasts that still practise long love, not noticing their tattered fur, not realizing they are victims of humanity's final cruelty? The air's worn whip will no longer electrify them, they will no longer roam their reserved territories nor toss and turn under the moon, unbothered above the ruins. They will sleep, the last of them, howling farewell amid mistreatments they do not comprehend, beneath blackened trees, like those foreseen in the *Inferno*'s thirteenth canto, except innocent. They too will condemn the guilty, indirect suicides, in this astonishing situation. But how can it be astonishing when there is no one to be astonished, no one left in that definitive night to rescue even a single word of the languages that failed to find their way from man's lips to his conscience, melted like a polar ice cap?

enthusiasm

May some god, even if by mistake, open the door to enthusiasm, day after day.

May innocence or cunning let me possess such a god.

Eulalia

I was a young girl and sitting at her feet – she was motionless in a rocking chair during her visit – I listened as she told the story of how Leonor had fallen from a horse-drawn carriage onto the dusty road, but no one had noticed. And I was there, in the middle of a lonely endless countryside beneath the blazing sun and I felt so thirsty... Did she realize she was planting in me a seed of fear and solitude? A stream of books flowed from her hands. The childhood library of a niece, now married, had gone to her house, and she loaned it to me little by little. Bringing and taking, bringing to my great joy, steadfastly taking, which left me maimed and deprived of an unexpected new love, an indispensable new-born friendship cut short: Verne, Dickens, Andersen, Scott. Today, all of a sudden, I can hear the echo of some elusive music in which I detect faint slivers of familiarity; as I scour my memory, I am convinced, always with a sense of melancholy, that this anxiety to seize what eludes me, this vague florescence of need and dispossession, has been with me since those remote vespertine sessions at Eulalia's feet, since those books were returned for eternity. The next evening after she had lent me *Genevieve of Brabant*[10] she asked, bending down intensely: 'Did it make you cry a lot?' She was caustic and patient. In return I gave her my nervous respect that often wavered but was drawn to that stream of books, to a possible oral story. I even revered as a sign of her wisdom, her gigantic bunions, the largest I have ever seen, and her Russian Leather perfume, the same until her death.

Eusebia

I do not know for how many years Eusebia had been living on that narrow street, not far from the sea, in a small house with a flowerbed out front. No sooner had I appeared in the house across from her than I received a visit. She correctly assumed they had not yet installed my telephone and offered to share hers with me. There was a serious problem with the terminals that limited the numbers allotted to each block; it took months to get one. I felt fortunate to have her kindness and made it a point to maintain a constant line of compensatory courtesies. Her true interests soon became clear, and I joined the other investing neighbors: between all of us we paid various halves. Eusebia did not have much money but also, like many people, she desired some form

---

[10] I still have an old Épinal print in which Genevieve sits with a boy at the entrance to a cave where she is forced to take shelter when the *perfidious* Golo's intrigues cause her husband to banish her from the court. Beside her a doe offers the boy its milk, though she presents him one of her own generous fountains, which he looks at as if unsure which he should choose. The story appears below it in verse, which I will not retell since it is well known, as is its slight resemblance to *Othello*. Seeing it when I am in Montevideo is a daily reminder of the person who first introduced me to it.

of power; by listening to conversations had with her phone, entering private worlds that would otherwise be out of reach behind neighboring walls, she hoped to acquire it. She liked to see, hear, and imagine perversities.

Not out of virtue but rather loneliness, out of a lack of voluntary listeners, she spouted her adverse opinions directly onto the accused. Despite my constant cautions that this telephone number was for matters of extreme urgency only, there was always a layout designer or some such person who found it more convenient to ring when he reached the newspaper whose literary page I organized back then, instead of asking around for my material. That would happen between nine and ten at night. Although she never ventured farther than her front door to summon me, I understood she might find that late hour inconsiderate and explained that those were the normal working hours for morning papers, but that she should tell them not to call, to no avail since she hoped to capture some juicy morsel of dialogue, relishing every opportunity to maliciously mention 'the men who called at night'.

One afternoon, as we were talking in her small, dimly lit living room, I noticed a point in the window lattice where light entered unimpeded thanks to an uncoincidental modification. I walked over to that luminous point: it offered a direct and disguised line of sight to the street and my front door. I suspected that once the radio plays were over, she would station herself there in hopes of being thrilled by some live drama. One night two or three married couples came round for a visit, something unexpected and scandalous in the eyes of the solitary spectator, but no doubt less so than seeing us exchange kisses goodbye.

The following day, dear Irma, impeccable and clever, who had worked for me for many years, listened with amused astonishment as she remarked: 'Merry life, sad death.' Even though I had established that Irma was to share in my privileges for the time we were without a telephone, she was also expected to pay, but in kind, that is, doing errands, small chores, which I was unable to prevent due to the fascination that despotism sometimes holds over simple people.

Her son, ungainly and getting on in age, whose father she never mentioned, visited her only very occasionally and accompanied by his matching wife. She had a grandson who was even less frequent. Since the world had not managed to charm Eusebia and because her prudent daughter-in-law was not usually around, the closest victim of her animosities was the obliging Marieta at the other end of the street. Angelic and unmarried, she spent her time giving injections to whoever asked her, helping her acquaintances, offering advice to the local children, or scolding them when a stray ball rattled her fence. Always occupied with something, she would refer to her converse and contentious neighbor without emotion or humor. Both recounted the ancient tale of their conflict whose trivialities were lost on me so that now I am unable to add any spicy detail to what remains of all this.

Eusebia had once been very beautiful, judging by the photos she liked to show us. Life had undoubtedly not kept the promises that for her such beauty assumed. She would later, in a meticulous act of scotomization, devote herself to combatting the things that upset her ego. One day she invited Irma over, who returned in a state of excitement never before seen: Eusebia had just gifted her a pair of earrings that she wore every now and then. I supposed that Irma's virtues had finally won her over. Afterwards I learned her generosity was the visible face of some serious problem with her daughter-in-law, who was beginning to be disinherited of what could have been hers.

I had already left Montevideo when my neighbors died, Eusebia being the first to go. I trust the prophesies of those most fed up with her were not fulfilled: 'There'll be no arms to carry her coffin through the door.' Despite everything, she was not that bad.

When I saw the house again years later, the tiny garden had disappeared and a young artist was living there. Her grandson perhaps? The gray door was decorated with something that resembled a body, life-size, amoeboid, and hideously mustard-colored. I felt relieved that I no longer lived there and did not have to see that each day. The previous owner, all told, was less aggressive.

exposition

Exposition, like exposure in the case of the first photographs, in part implies stillness, a suspension of potential change, an almost mortuary process, a viewing *à la américaine*. Exposition does not modify what is being exposed, it detains it, mummifies it. And those who see it, are they at all altered? Meanwhile, the term continues to be applied to art exhibits, even if some have entered the twenty-first century with entirely untraditional styles. Exploring the term's mortuary dimension awakens my recollections of the funereal, the tragic, and my memory does not waver: Austin, 1990-something, a curious, unexpected exposition, exhumatory to the highest degree: projects by Soviet architects – the last of the Stalinist period – which were never realized. Not only were they unrealizable – they almost all were – but also incommunicable in their time, not without braving great and obvious risks.

It is normal to exhibit work submitted in response to some call that, in the case of architectural projects, anticipates the realization of one of them, the winner, whether in justice or not. However, the projects in this exposition were born out of painful spontaneity, solitary, defeated, and without hope, secretly bound by a shared anxiety divided amongst members of a segment of society, whom I assume were silent and fearfully disunited. Faced with the horrible demand for an outdated style, inhibited by the predictable prohibition of certain names, freedoms, and aesthetic solutions, their answers began taking shape, each one from its obligatory solitude and in secret.

But human singularities arise even beneath the violence that a society can wield. While some of these protest-projects exuded desperation, others ventured down the path of dark humor and irony. We also cannot rule out, in one case, a certain naïveté that thought it possible to sell us a pup. They were not intended for the isolated individual, as if there were no place for them even in the deepest recesses of the human record. Hence the walls exhibited glorified monuments or gardens from the Rococo, imaginable returns to the past, as if the past were the only possible illusion, aesthetic on the surface but moral at heart: proof of the natural distrust of the future, the eroded hopes, and the murk of a horizon where enthusiasm has fallen into definitive night. Perhaps, because of how intensely reactionary any revolution's art ultimately opts to be, these gardens proposed a style of undefined antiquity, like an old-fashioned folktale. The modest arches, the manicured hedges and small trees, the sad lampposts and arbors, offered up by the abolished architect like oblations to the irrational Moloch of political reason, did not even suggest a flowering spring but a perennial Siberia.

Many years have passed since I read the somber truth of those papers, aged and yellowed, their edges tattered as often occurs when stored in rolls. Time reduced the number of messages in my memory to the most striking one of them all. At the end of the visit, an inverted skyscraper in cross section strived not for elevation and light but instead descended into the earth. That deep well drafted in black ink had many floors and those floors had black doors and windows, sealing up that atrocious tomblike space. There was no room in it for the irony of a sparse empty garden, distant in time and space, eighteenth-century and French. Only the absolute despair of a smothered collective life, all purpose, all meaning lost, save for the faint hope of that message placed inside that bottle and tossed into the sea or buried, finally reaching some stretch of future where it could be received, understood, sympathized, though all its senders are undoubtedly no longer above ground. At least they were spared from confirming the now known futility of so much suffering.

eye

A humble homage to Christian Morgenstern

The firm eye was always open wide,
faithful keyhole granting its lock sight,
despite the fury it felt inside
that not everything was at its height.

Suddenly someone, all cares aside,
with a key turned its world to night,
which the irritated eye decried
as pillage and a personal slight.

Neither visionary nor cross-eyed
nor prone to tears or to pick a fight,
who would dare its perfect view blindside
by performing this optical sleight?

No one deems it an ungiving guide
or narrow in its perspective. Might-
n't the door lock believe it had died
if the eye had not shown it the light?

F

fire

Fire lurks in every corner, waiting for you without occupying any visible place. But those with an ear for it expect it in the rustle of dried leaves when autumn sets its haphazard red ablaze, like a flame that rides the wind and engulfs the ivy on the walls.

Fire is more committed to nearby materials than water, and its relationship with them is definitive. Water floods, but it is willing to abandon what it conquers. Fire, if it springs forth, will flourish and must be flogged, persecuted, there where it lies hidden, if we do not want to yield to its dominion. Despite what one might think, its adversary is not water but sand, dry scorching sand. There is no worse enemy than a kindred soul. But some of fire's sacredness is passed onto the burnt material. The cinders of the old chestnut tree that in some places are lit on Christmas Eve, the yule log, are kept as a relic to ward off storms with what igneous forces they still contain.

Do not oppose it. Kindly respect its boundaries. Crepitations are its way of welcoming you into its conversation. Join in its rhythm, identify yourself in an act of love with time that explodes among sparks, accelerated. It will give you sanctuary.

It is both possessed and a possessor. It exercises such strong authority over anyone who confronts it that you cannot avoid its governance, for as long as it lasts. To be entitled to fire, you are expected to feed it, toss it a twig at the very least. This is one of the few forms of magic, one of the few vertigos that civilization has not managed to eradicate. This is the ritualistic gesture for the inevitable combustion of any judgment you may have when you approach it.

flight

The birds are the first to fade from sight,
the trees fall into a single shadow,
the earth transforms into an empty board,
smoke becomes cloud.
Now in my high-speed seat I should like
to ask for a future like a sweet juice,
minutes to steadily sip it,
for an attendant to refill it, friendly.

flood

The sound of a falling drop repeats in the central and, until that moment, silent night, it persists, one plash chases another, it changes in quality, it is no longer a collision with a smooth ceramic surface, it grows less precise when the following drop meets more water and those that come after now sink without a sound, accepted into the liquid current and sands rise in the calcined silence and a long, green valley filters through them, in it the Waters of Merom swell, surrounded by marshes and rushes and they spill over and are the source of the Jordan and high above the sky is deeply blue and overwhelms the small donkey carrying a woman wrapped in a mantle, also blue, hunched under the terrible sun and over a boy, while beside her a man walks upright and gives them shade...

fungi

That Sunday my Aunt Débora had lent my sixth-grade teacher her Chevrolet, something she did sometimes perhaps to spare herself the headaches its defiant motor caused her or to put it to the test in other hands. We were going to the park that I will continue to call Durandeau, resisting the national and forgetful obsession to change the civic nomenclator according to partisan winds. Weekends were exempted from pedagogy and its contaminations. But that one seemed like it was going to be different, since Pía was there... My shyness kept me quiet in a corner of the automobile.

We finally crossed into the greenish light, shielded from the high sun by canopies of eucalyptus and pine, into the cushioned crackle of fallen leaves, and into the repeated cadence sounding in the distance, resonant and somewhat mysterious like swaying melancholic bells, of the swings or the iron rings released by the children running in circles, dangling from them to briefly soar through the air.

A confusion of people, sand, and soil surrounded the swings and rings. There were no trees. There were thus no mushrooms. And so we were to continue walking, leaving that place far behind because fungi were our only interest, our sole activity. Pía was well versed in them. It amazed me how, not just indifferent to the swings but also to the spectacular trees, the areas blanketed in pine needles where you could roll about softly, without danger, lush with beautiful, fragrant pinecones, she headed towards a specific point as if guided by the divining rod of a parched rhabdomancer. There, digging with precise tenderness, she uncovered a plump family of delicious milk-caps. The two of us on our knees, like in an act of ritual adoration, she spoke, distinguishing between species, singing definitions, praising shapes, explaining their method of reproduction, joyously inhaling their smell of humus, protecting the spores. The circle in which the mushrooms were gathered no doubt corresponded to a mental image. To prevent it from being disturbed, that mandala was given solicitous treatment. Enclosed with twigs, hidden with leaf litter, it became a *temenos*, a center where our energies united in the creation of a defense system. We needed to protect them from the clumsy enemy milling about. We worshipped the mushrooms out of love for Nature, and though I had not yet discovered the dittany, I soon realized the gratuitous and almost divine splendor of those mysterious beings. Naturally, we paid little attention to the imperfect fungi, deuteromycetes, saprophytes, parasites (neither good nor bad) of other beings, or to *Candida albicans* or cephalosporins. Only those that possessed a certain vegetal and visible appeal.

But the forest was teeming with dark hordes. They ran unhinged and unceremoniously, yelling, with primitive children who also scoured the area. We felt them arrive like the *Abade chacurra*, that whirlwind of vertiginous, eternal dogs, trailed by the priest condemned for interrupting mass to go hunting. They searched for fungi to devour them. They discovered them amid screams and ripped them from the ground without a second thought, without seeing if they were fully ripe, if along with the Great Mother Mushroom they were not killing the little baby mushrooms, culinarily uninteresting, that the species needed for survival.

We were environmentalists – though I did not know it – and they were the enemies to be hated. Our defeat at the hands of the barbarians was signified by the destruction of our covered fortress: the innocent structure that Pía had erected a week earlier, leaving behind certain markers to recognize it, laid to waste during their definitive and improvident extermination.

In reality, the variety of fungi was limited and so was what I was capable of learning. After the names of their few parts, after distinguishing the good from the bad, the edible from the slightly toxic and one that was indeed poisonous but easily identifiable once its color and pattern had been demonized, after knowing about the ones that grow on dead tree trunks, as hard as the wood itself and not gastronomically tempting to anyone, yet beautiful with their unfurled fan in velvety red, orange, and gold, I would have considered our class concluded and run off to enjoy the swings abandoned by the enemy mobs. But night was falling, and it was time to leave. The drive back would be slow because now those same masses (who filled no more than a handful of cars) would plague the road home.

Toward the end of the school year and faced with the high school entry exam, Pía assigned oral presentations to review the subjects. Of course, mine was on fungi. I diligently studied them in our botany textbook. As I did, I no doubt again sensed the perfume of the eucalyptus trees, the crackle of the pine needles, and the melancholic ringing of the swings, enduring and distant, resonated in my memory. None of that was discernible in what I presented. A disappointed Pía said she had expected something else. It was clear to me that school and life were things that occurred on distinct planes. Was I supposed to allude to that mystery, to unspoken things, secret and important: the fight against evil? How could I talk about that in front of the class? For me, fungi were just a pretext. Or am I wrong? Were they not my reserves, my adventure? We did not understand each other and that was an early disappointment.

Soon after, Pía would be my high school biology teacher. Over the years, now also an adult myself, I often ran into her, we would talk, she told me about her life, married and happy, then about her unfortunate widowhood, but never again about fungi.

G

garlic

    Garlic, enemy of peaceful digestion,
    marauder of the sulfurs of hell,
    only by punishment of boiling oil
    can you reach redemption and paradise.

gato

I

We say *gato* and, prone to simplification, we imagine nothing more than different coats, different colors, the slender figure of an Egyptian cat ready to be eternalized in stone, the Persian's sky-blue eyes, a portly Angora inside its particular silky aura. But whoever presumes to spend any time with cats is bound to notice their great variety of psychological subtleties and realize they are immeasurable. The Spanish language has included a few: that they are clever and cautious in the word *marrullero* (smooth-tongued), apparently derived from the verb *marrullar* (to purr), a cat's snore, a cross between *maullar* (to meow) and *arrullar* (to coo). Also, that they like to lie beside the fire, and thus metaphorically, the pot typically found there was called a *marmita* (marmite), from *marlou* and *mite*, familiar pet names for French *chats*, similar to the hypocorisms *morro* and *morrongo* for the Spanish *gato*. However, they are not responsible for the *gatuperios* (ruses) that, taking the downward path – or cathode – of a hasty deduction, we might blame on them.

Finding shelter in language, cats allowed monkeys and dogs, sheep, donkeys, horses, bulls, lions, boars, eagles, indistinct birds, and a still vaster array of fauna to benefit from the topographical intuitions that determined the filling of (sometimes secondary) spaces in paintings. European Medieval and Renaissance art largely ignored the house cat. Amidst the extravagant gestures of Brueghel's peasants, the cat sleeps or has slipped away, prudent in the land of Cockaigne, unafraid though surrounded by an unhealthy curiosity to ascend the calvary, ready to escape these inclemencies to the peacefulness of a pillow, in the darkness of a Flemish interior, in the domesticity of a Chardin, in the world without visible anxieties of the Naïfs.

II

The noble cat
saunters in a fit of somnolence
to the usual pillow and takes his rest
at the center of his kingdom,
augur of the order of things.
His half-shut eyes
keep everything safe
inside his speculative perimeters.
He is content in his concentric warmth.
He ignores, almost humanlike,
that he only exists with respect to the Other.

III

Any parapet proffers them aid,
their commandments are calmness,
discretion and disdain
and even the routine of their routes,
the majesty of their stealth.

From on high where they reign
free from volatile moods,
always to the ground they look,
never to the sky, like men,
to a vain and distant dream.

Multiple active cats,
varied in fur and manner,
solemnly surveil my labors,
the turbid story of my days.
Am I deserving of any hope?

IV

A cat made for winters and pillows,
its clairvoyant eye phosphoric,
its muffling fur electric,

though it tolerates unconsented names
– Kiki, Micifuz, Berenice,
Rabinagrobis, Miruz, Nekomata –
it can, like a hostage, discard it,
precipitous cursive master
of lightning-fast license,

and climb the milky stairway
to the meowing rooftops
where it can be as it pleases, a cat.

V

C'est vrai, Cingria / qu'en regardant la prunelle d'un chat / on peut savoir l'heure ?

geography

When geography appeared as a subject in my field of learning, I took it as a pleasant, unexpected gift and accepted it, thanks to my propensity for confusion. Before that, in a deliciously prescientific stage, it had dressed the bones of my school lessons with a bit of flesh as a result of the vague, picturesque notions I harvested here and there and arranged into a sort of diorama, undoubtedly beautiful and incoherent, in which Patagonians walked among glaciers, and Tutankhamen (who was not yet a boy and had the head of Ramses) led me down a partially collapsed tunnel to his pyramid, not very far from the Nile's headwaters protected by a magnificent forest where cockatoos watched lions from the lianas.

These charming images had as much to do with geography as furious Orlando's actions did with the history that included Frederick Barbarossa. I found them by reading *One Thousand and One Nights*, Fénelon's *Telemachus* (abridged), a hedonistic personal selection from the encyclopedias of *Tesoro de la juventud*, Hans Christian Andersen, and infinite grazing, which I have as little memory of as I do the purées that accompany my daily meals. There was also the unforgettable *Summa Artis* devoted to Egypt. Later, more seriously, if possible, came the journeys of Nils Holgersson and Verne, so much Verne. My world was happy, eco-friendly, and believed in progress. All this without contradictions. Save for the 'burning sands of the desert', an incombustible phrase plucked from who knows where, everything else that was not 'wine-dark sea' was forest, glades to be exact, the backdrop for galloping Knights of the Round Table, Percival, and Robin Hood.

My topography, so fanciful that it could have come from the travel journal of some flitting fairy, acquired a more realistic quality when De Amicis' *Heart* brought me down to worlds of human suffering with *From the Apennines to the Andes* or *The Little Vidette of Lombardy*.

The inevitable arrival of more-scientific knowledge was not too harsh or traumatic by the grace and work of a gentle teacher, Don Horacio Ferrer Pérez. To this day, I am grateful to him for accepting, and even showing interest, in the ideas I rattled off when called upon by surprise to give a class on Africa without it having yet occurred to me to study the topic in the assigned source. With an audaciousness born of panic, I organized my memories of *A Captain at Fifteen* or *The Children of Captain Grant*. Drawing from these books, since Verne had had the charming idea they should take place in Africa, the description of giant termite nests replaced the required information – unknown to me and certainly complicated – concerning its orographical system with the locations, names, and elevations of mountains as well as volcanoes, if there were any. As I carried on without interruption, my confidence grew and my account gained verisimilitude and a certain expositive vigor, unbothered by the fact that my version, almost celestial (in honor of Larrea), was defiantly deviating from the radical conventions of the textbooks.

Nevertheless, orthodox geography held indelible emotions here and there, like Vesuvius and its lava and a living, breathing Pompei that in a few terrifying instants is transformed into a museum-city filled with contorted statues. I was as interested in what existed visibly as what might exist submerged beneath the ash and earth or below the water, like Atlantis. I began to hear about archaeological revelations, though far away, sadly. I could also fantasize about the days before the headwaters of the Nile had been discovered.

Soon enough the technocrats would come along with their ambitions to convert geography, still capable of enchantment, into a statistical wasteland pervaded by human migrations, hunger, and threats to the future, and in whose mountains, plagued by cable cars and transmission towers, nobody would expect a visit from the Roc bird or the Abominable Snowman. And the time for dreaming was over.

It is not surprising, then, that geography has again become a space abandoned as unhealthy. The always entertaining Savater – a delightful virtue to have – recalls that during his visit to Villahermosa, Mexico and its packed hotels, while they had not offered him a '*media con limpio*' (half a bed shared with a clean guest) as they used to in the inns of yore, he did have to share a room with a young engineer whose casual knowledge improved when he was enlightened as to the location of Spain, now without viceroyalties.

In the past such a void of information would have horrified me. Today I see the waters have receded many levels, to the point where I fear the skeletons of many forgotten corpses will be revealed. I have read with shocking disbelief the answers of American university students who do not know their country's state capitals and barely know that to its south lies Mexico and then an indistinct expanse where *hic sunt leones*. And let us not forget the politicians who learn via invasions. To be honest, I sometimes also find myself accusing maps of being too provisional in order to exonerate myself when I cannot place a city at the edges of Europe or a new country in Africa.

Will geography soon become an arcane concept without merits? What territories will welcome the wandering dreams of those deprived? An amorphous magma of numbers and graphs is going to scare off the once leisurely, curious, light-footed travelers who will now miss out on the first part of the fun: embroidering over the early idea they had of reality before correcting or corroborating it. Geographical ignorance will serve as an excuse to cling tight to one's monad, to be more obtusely nationalistic, placing the knowledge that does survive – historical, artistic, literary, or whatever else – at greater risk of jettison, not having anywhere to put it.

With the nescience of mythologies, and I am referring merely to Greek and Roman, both foundational for the Europeanized West, a cupola of infinite resonances has collapsed, leaving people semi-deaf and semi-illiterate in bulk. *The* [entertaining] *Marriage of Cadmus and Harmony*, by Calasso, brought an unexpected resurrection of the myths that through a subterranean vein nourish or should nourish the aridity of a world that is losing its deepest illusions. But they alone will not be able to right this disaster. To how many winged graduates of certain universities I know does Mount Parnassus or Boeotia ring a bell, except for those enthusiasts of crosswords, a great cultural aid in times like these? Nowadays I look benevolently on those creatures in cafés, airplanes, or waiting rooms whom I once rejected when seeing them squander their treasured free time repeating the exhausted combinations of these exercises in patience, where the Obi constantly flows and the scops owl sings. I applaud them for engaging their intellect a little and learning new terms, although they will certainly never have the opportunity to use them outside those gridded cages for dried mandrakes.

And do not tell me that globalization and mass media are increasing information more than ever seen before. Its frequency, yes, which is not the same thing. Besides, is it so important to inform us of what immediately becomes a forgotten past?

giraffe

It is perhaps the most amusing of the animals that, according to Vasari, *la natura fa per istranezza*.[11] The tender individuality in the image of the opossum, zariguëya, or tlacuache with all her young aboard is mostly thanks to her obedient offspring, aligned atop her back like passengers on a crowded bus, their little tails clutching the long tail their mother curls over them toward her head.[12] It is a true act of familial

---

[11] Nature makes out of eccentricity.

[12] We cannot even trust the drawings that, with presumed accuracy, accompany observations in the natural sciences. Now I know that the first note on the opossum was made by Maria Sibylla Merian, German artist (Frankfurt, eighteenth century) who had the good fortune of seeing the little animal in Suriname and reproduced it faithfully, just as she had seen it with its children on its back. Subsequent illustrators, far removed from the model, reworked the veracious drawing and used their imagination to exceed nature itself, to my mistaken fascination. The admirable J. J. Audubon escapes unscathed, once again, having sketched the Virginia opossum with its baby peeking out from its marsupial pouch. Because the opossum is an everyday occurrence in Austin, like the raccoon or mapache, I

teamwork. Anyway, a long tail, the source of people's unsympathetic view and the comparisons they make between it and the unalluring rat, is less preternatural than a long neck, and its South American origin – does anyone deny it? – is more modest than the Africa of the giraffe. In the giraffe, man satisfies his tendency for greater exoticism as well as his taste for excess and disproportion. It compensates for his weariness with the harmony he believes defines him. A giraffe was a sumptuous, sultanic gift; Florence's Signoria was graced with one, very large and very beautiful and pleasing, prominent in a shipment of various animals. The occasion was important enough for the historian Luca Landucci to record its appearance: 11 November 1487, and for many painters to use it to enrich the depths and distances of their paintings with the unbelievable, newly discovered figure. (Dürer would prefer the impressive rhinoceros and its artic-ulated armor.) That giraffe survived the first winter and five winters more; it did not however die its own death, it did not die of exile, that is, of nostalgia, or of pneumonia, but instead broke its neck when passing through a doorway it would have never encountered in its native jungle.

The giraffe, a 'hieroglyph of truth in the animal kingdom' in Charles Fourier's view, is an angelic creature; I have not seen its name spoken among those

---

have had the chance to see it up close in the houses of friends who are practically offended by my interest: they do not support the ani-mal's promenades through their yards, an almost domestic compan-ion to the cat, whose food it partakes of without conflict. I looked with delight at its light gray face, coming to a point at its snout, its two intense black eyes looking back at me unalarmed. I noticed no signs of its marsupiality; it could have been a male or female momen-tarily freed of its young.

performing tasks in the legendary hells. Its long neck affords elevated grazing that spares it from fighting with other animals over sustenance or causes it to bow down with more humility than any other. On the list of wonders with which Jehovah challenged Job, we find the ibis and the rooster, the deer and the onager, the ostrich and the stork, the hawk and the horse, the ox and indirectly, the locust, and Behemoth and Leviathan – the rhinoceros and the whale – his most baroque and compact creations, but it makes no mention of the elegant giraffe. Discreet Jehovah, who wished not to boast in the presence of the complainer by citing the culmination of his ingenuity.

ghost

Someone who having been told many times, 'Die!' insists on living.

grandfather

Photographs pretend to be immutable images. Some perhaps are. The one of my grandfather is not. For a time, it never occurred to me to doubt its constancy. Had someone asked me about it, I would have benefitted earlier from that closer look and forced reflection, gaining the slight amazement and inner transformation, minor or major, that any new perspective provides. I have had this photograph with me for years. Looking at it is to remember the good and the bad of my lineage, although not all of it can be attributed to this grandfather. Like everyone, I have another, and two grandmothers, eight great-grandparents of both sexes, sixteen great-great-grandparents. I was not very inquisitive as a child; I was every bit as distracted as one can manage to be when nobody is insisting we kneel at the altars of the familial empyrean, immersing us head first in domestic history. And so, they were engulfed by the nebula, the misty infinity that is the barathrum of our ancestors. But we know they were there, to dilute the responsibilities of their children and allow me to imagine that something original and individual still exists in each of us, the result of interweaving others' diluted natures. Without discounting possible, lateral occurrences whose fruits secretly alter family trees.

Back to my grandfather Félix, my father's father. He had what is usually considered to be a Roman head: high forehead, straight nose, a mouth neither protruding nor recessed; also blue eyes that only Uncle Pericles, my father, and, through him, I would inherit, in accordance with some of Mendel's laws, as accurate as those of that villain Malthus. And a good head of hair, a moustache and beard consistent with the fashion back then, although the men of that period, preoccupied with building a country – in the case of these Italian travelers, a different country, far from their own – and a family, were perhaps unconcerned with such superficialities.

Dignified but not sullen, with a hint of a smile that was more patient than happy, he stands against a neutral, gray background where a mirror hangs gleaming. No fin-de-siècle house plants, no wallpaper with pomegranates or peacock feathers, no imaginative undulating landscapes across a painted curtain, which cheapened the most Proustian elegancies. This gave that snapshot taken at the start of the century a very modern air, at least very 1950. I suppose it was its domestic quality that cast doubt on its date. In those days, recording an image required a professional, comings or goings, a certain amount of production. Long after my grandfather's death, my father and Uncle Manlio had photographic machines, elegant models with bellows that did not require a tripod but because of their base seemed to call for some form of horizontal support. Was one of them the photographer? Had a terrace at the house in Prado provided that indistinct background that offered so little stimulation to my imagination overcome with reconstructive curiosity?

Could it have been because of his calm demeanor that the changes began invading his surroundings first? I noticed an aureole of bluish haze around my grand-father, an opalescence like that which affects certain blind eyes. Its emergence isolated the dark figure, making the vague reality around him even more so. Space and time suffered this transmutation. Space, more unseizable; time, more imprecise; temporal determinations, always sinuous. Distant things are always held in some eternity into which we suddenly fall, effortlessly – Alice's gentle descent down the well – or enter standing in a doorway from where we can see the suspended gestures, the shadowless lights of a bygone conversation, deliciously lethargic and indis-tinct, occurring in a space seemingly guarded from all calamities but in which, alas, we never manage to set foot. The photograph transforms and carries off the little information I can seize hold of, since I was not born in time to meet the model.

The obvious link to my grandfather was my grandmother. She must have spent her youth tremen-dously occupied with the precursory steps and birth of fourteen children and the rearing of twelve and was active and did not indulge in reminiscence. She died at the age of ninety-six, after a swift decline, sitting in an armchair and just as she was trying to recall whether or not she had already had her after-lunch coffee. It was time for them to relieve her of command and of the world. Today I regret not asking her about her married life. But given my age then, I doubt she would have taken me into her confidence. Though she had countless stories sprinkled with biting humor about the not-so-open field of her relationships, the juicy details of her childhood and early adolescence were interrupted and changed tone when she reached her marriage. It was delayed because of my grandfather's adherence to his principles: Garibaldian and a Mason, he waited two years until the creation of the civil registry so as not to suffer what he called the holy gallows. That was the official version. But as I enjoy imagining the other side of the moon, I can think of a less austere explanation: perhaps Félix Vitale d'Amico, arriving somehow in the small town of Nuestra Señora del Rosario, completed his law studies at the University of Palermo and granted himself two years of freedom before what was predictably expected of him: a family of his own, the move to the capital, and the laborious fabric of a responsible career.

From that point on I only have a handful of anecdotes about that career and his life: the described and adjectivized client, recognized by one of the children who opened the door to him and announced at the top of their lungs, with the keen memory of youth: 'Papa, the criminal is here,' causing the caller to disappear; the foundation stone for the monument to one Genovese Christopher Columbus, an occasion that seems to have been sufficiently lavish for my grandfather to arrive by carriage. The monument, which was never erected, was to be located in the Port of Montevideo. (It is not hard to imagine the Spanish colony's diligences in sabotaging the project, anticipating a century later the debates on the five hundred years of his discovery.) I will limit the stories that occurred behind closed doors to one that, while trivial, gives some idea of his severity: one of his daughters, a young girl at the time, refused a strawberry that was offered to her in the kitchen. When it was time for dessert and those strawberries were brought out now fully prepared, her father did not allow her to eat them, transforming that trivial misstep into a lifelong lesson. Since certain rigors, which I took no pleasure in registering, can be taken from the pages of inherited pedagogy, whenever I looked at those revered portraits I would think, very much to myself, how fortunate it was that generations came to earth in successive waves of time and that my fairy godmother, whose existence I never doubted, had cared for my date of arrival so as to spare me the inflexibilities that floated throughout our household tales.

Oh, what many and diverse, clouded things emerge from the surface of a cloudy portrait!

H

Hamlet (News for)
Today aunt mother and father uncle
rule over us,
the kingdom regresses
to the rank of mercenary province.
Every border smells of soldiery.

Acids seep into the ear
not of a sad king alone,
of adolescent kings by the thousands,
of men who would be kings
if not for this empoisoned rhapsody of lies.

But as you know, Prince,
when the southerly wind blows against the people,
the cobwebs fly off
and despite how dark everything around us may be
we can clearly see the handsaws, the hawks.

1967

heritage

I am fascinated by nonhuman animals, perhaps for hereditary reasons. An aunt who collaborated with the wise naturalist Arechavaleta, creator of Montevideo's Botanical Garden, died before I was born. Not only do I bear her name, but I also inherited her things: books and furniture that I lived and breathed, disregarding my grandmother's rigorous project of sacralization. Short on animals, my childhood was nourished by the infinite zoological anecdotes that constituted almost the entirety of my aunt's brief history: the tame sparrow perched on the tip of her pen as she wrote; the shoes abandoned the necessary amount of time for a silkworm whose mother had woven its cocoon into the hospitable angle between the sole and the heel to undergo its metamorphosis in peace; the drawers of her night table fallen into disuse because some specimen under examination had strayed from its originally assigned box and decided on its own place of residence. And risk free because the stories never included retaliation on the part of Aunt Ida. I learned about the dramatic period when she shared her bedroom with some white mice – that multiplied – to save them from vagrant cats and were detested by the rest of the family, faithful instead to canines and felines. And to the caged ñacurutú, a great horned owl always ruffling angrily at everything that was not her. Among her/my furniture there was a large, closed bookcase with dozens of identical little white boxes. They held treasures from the three kingdoms: berries, kermes scales, popcorn kernels, chrysalises, hymenopterans, lepidopterans, a starfish, a seahorse, a hummingbird nest, miniscule and perfect, and stones that I loved for their color, shine, or patterns, or for their names, like feldspar or orpiment. There was even an authentic gold nugget among this heritage trove, out of place beside several little, turquoise-colored eggs, all empty. A bronze microscope presided over that desiccated paraphernalia. With it, I grew accustomed to extracting as much ecstasy from almost stagnant waters as I would later from kaleidoscopes. I had not yet developed claws to defend myself when everything was expropriated by an uncle who was a doctor. His patients, perversely worsening in the middle of the night (an interval during which he placed his Hippocratic Oath like this, between parentheses, and turned a deaf ear to any phone calls), gradually ceased to consult him until he was forced to earn a living with less harmful abandon. First, he taught classes on natural history. Later, he considered this to be similar to geography – why not? – and began teaching it while trying to learn its rudiments at the expense of my minimal library: he seized a beautiful copy of *Geografía Pintoresca* I had been gifted and gutted it for its maps, their surreptitious presence in class acting as a substitute for the science that was reluctant to illuminate him. He was not covetous of other books. I swear I never saw him frequent them beyond the minimum required by his profession, though they were not lacking in our house. This spared the other line of posthumous benefits that Aunt Ida had imparted to me. While the boxes and microscope were relocated to her brother's 'consulting' room where nothing disturbed their dark peace, I retained possession of her books, which I enjoyed later on. In those early years, Fabre (Jean-Henri) perpetuated my lost museum. Drawn to Calpe's covers, matte but with sharp colors, I discovered a singular style of the epic in Fabre's works before I ever did in Homer or El Cid. Jules, his son and field assistant, was my only imaginary childhood friend during those golden afternoons he spent patiently observing beetles, spiders, or ants.

Hernández, Felisberto

With his back to a purgatory of piano keys, Felisberto sees Pegasi that look like him fly past, he penetrates dark veils with his luminotechnical eyes. He has bridled his initial temptation to caress the feathers of the angels, the cloth of the tunics, the frightened faces of the newly arrived, but he still silently sidles up to cumuli and nimbi and blows away the billows to see what lies beneath, behind the backs of whoever might be monitoring for indiscretions. Sometimes they have him steer the boat that shuttles between East and West. He complies with gravity while dreaming he is traveling between islands of plants. Bowed in cheerful obedience, he touches morbid inexistence, the impalpable atoms, hoping to divine what substance they once composed. Other times he looks toward the earth, remembers thinking that 'space and air were cruel' for him when he was down there learning the submissive art of survival, which now he can forget, and leans against collapsing balconies. Like a key to the final terraces, he put the struggle with his work ahead of himself and everything. It still weighs on him to think about it and he wonders what they have done with all that consumed so much of him, what they will do, what they have not done, and what they will not do, and because now he knows every language, he mutters: *J'en ai marre,*[13] softly, since at certain altitudes agitation produces profound

---

[13] I'm fed up.

vortexes of astral dust. Juan Emar, that Chilean also
uprooted from the spirit of the times, is moved from
a distance, the one that separates them, and nods to
him in implied friendship and shared patience.

Hicacos

Out of profound love for the moment
light lowers its final defenses,
boards fly off, Solomonic columns,
the battens, the barrenness, fly off.
The clouds bowed down before the night,
before the facts of a fading dream.
A glimmer of Veronese green,
dazzling vestige of the darkened world,
fills the painting where one day I will
see someone else, myself, not yet here.

history

I

A viscous sensation, oscillating between vertigo and
lethargy, appears when pointing out to a group of
adolescents the specular symmetry we find between
the first Hellenics and us, twenty centuries before and
after Christ. In between – demented compression –
occurs all history, all culture, all terror, the uncontrollable whirlwinds, the frenzied clockmaking, the crazy
machines that start to run forward in good working
order but are beset, suddenly, by the delirium of
retreat and seem to reassess and yet reiterate, overcome
horrors and render them simple inept blueprints for
the increasingly greater catastrophes that civilization
procures.

History,
wreath of horror,
worn wheel teetering,
tireless
tom-tom,
river summoning to war,
fiery reverse side of a smooth sheet,
topological confusion of serpents.

humor

Many species of humor exist: the most subtle is the
one that acclimates itself to mystery.

I

I

Complex Chinese brevity: '*I* refers to everything unseen and everything that encompasses everything. Everything heard and not understood is called *I*. What is darkest and what is lightest is called *I*. What is undefinable and contains all definitions, what is without origin and what gives origin to everything is called *I*.' The *I*, for us a succinct letter constricted by its own limits – with difficulties sinking and rising but always on the verge of entering the bastion of the numbers, at the risk of planetary collision – in China amasses with astonishing accumulative elasticity a profusion of meanings that resemble divine attributes. It is the opposite of a chrysanthemum or a peony, a jade Han chimera, a funerary Tang statue, a Song winged lion, places where curves prevail; nevertheless, it manages to subtilize its minimal ridges in favor of vastness in order to comprise everything – must everything possible reach us through it? – like a hieroglyphic of indecipherable mysteries.

Iceland

At eight o'clock at night I watch as the sun's burning circle descends, slow and without setting. It seems to be checking, the prudent elder, to see if its circumstances might mean the imaginable cold of the sea that sits before me. Later it will submerge unhurried, with discretion, because its absence, for a good while, will change nothing.

Not the landscape, which depends on it so much, nor the light. The sun has disappeared, but the light, autonomous, continues unvarying. Hours will pass and the blue sky will continue its indelible existence and the four of us, Hoffy and Pál and Enrique and I, will have left that remote beach, and the crisp cameo will remain in relief behind us, the golden sand in back and the thin layer of green grass that adds color here. At some point the sunset will begin like low tide.

Is there a better symbol of what we should aspire to? Once we are invisible, submerged, leave an enduring light that might possibly ease someone's strain.

inclemency

There is no use sighing; autumn has come. The dry leaves fall with such intensity that we walk always between their crunch and their powder. Sometimes a veritable windstorm of yellow envelops us, halfway between happiness and the cold. Inch by inch we discover how it gradually acquires its intentionality as a shared season, yard by yard we wander the space that now has an air of stained glass with first offerings. We take out scarves of acceptance, books to match its rhythm, anthologies of projects, we eat fruits, chocolate, mouths. But the space grows increasingly narrow and harsh, and between one caress and another we watch the roof from where the leaves, in greater and greater numbers, continue to fall.

ingenuity

The markets and also many homes are filled with seemingly irrefutable objects. We might call them late-ripening fruit draped in divine genius. Each time, we believed we were seeing an invention, placed under our pillow, from a discreet hand whose vision reaches beyond the night's top floor. Simple and magical like an egg, each one of them appears to be the solution – what took so long? – to one of those frustrating, recurring problems that make up the tyranny of everyday life. Many of those monuments to ingenuity crumble the moment we try them. A spring gets stuck if we decide to put it to the test, a coupling leaks the liquid it should retain, a procedure proves much more complicated and laborious than the one it was meant to simplify. With each disappointment we learn to distrust absolute solutions.

Human ingenuity not only manifests itself in objects: also in ideas, examples, relationships, theories. Sometimes these constitute an ensemble that is brilliant, hygienic, chrome-plated, and comfortable in appearance. I know someone whose argumentative aplomb is dazzling. He isolates a line from a long book he need not read or directs his attention to an abandoned fragment of our vast reality – the awful reality that could refute him – and erects a quick creation that looks to be a diadem of good sense. If it were a bathroom, we would soon discover that hot water pours from where the cold water should and the drains regurgitate convulsively; but we would not be able to protest. He would assure us that, obviously, it is better this way, or he would ask if we had expected music to flow from the tap.

Everything about him is expedient: *beware of Greeks bearing gifts*. He is ignorant of the frontiers; he knows his town well, or so he thinks, and is certain the rest of the world is a reiteration of it. If he ventures out, he carries it with him and compares with ease. He believes there is one model. That is enough for him. He believes his knowledge is sufficient; he finds other people's knowledge irritating. Sometimes he grows distressed when there are evident setbacks. But he is an optimist, and his electroplating gaze restores the various nearby minutiae with a thin coat of equalizing gold, even if reality contradicts him. He is a living contradiction. I think within his *ipsissimum* he is a despot, due to an excess of rationalism. But he is essentially good and capable of placing his powers at the service of causes that were also once golden. His ingenuity is his act of love, his reason for being, for himself and for others. It is not his fault that reality – the society around him and almost all of the people who comprise it – is not at the level of that act of love.

Ingres

In Ingres, 'a man from China lost in the streets of Athens', I accept the tenacity of his blues, the satin, sometimes ochre and golden like a church by Saenredam, the flesh, added ingredients to orange blossoms, at random and by law, that rhapsodic darning of odalisques in his room, waxing moons, the proclamations of unaltered beauty, alter egos of one another; the glazed, agglutinated nudes of *The Turkish Bath* and others; his *Mlle. Rivière*, this time white silk, gloved in singed yellow, light blue sky and river, with its very verisimilar green in the distance, so many happy portraits of seemingly happy women. I accept it all and enjoy it save for the Greek programs, the agitated agoras, the mythologies – with all that they nourish – the Roman heroes, the stories in bodies, the draped dramas, the troubadourish Gothic or the troubadouresque Romanticism of his version of the *Inferno*'s Canto V, with a Paolo who resembles Tenniel's amusing lizard and a husband who emerges, Victorian, from behind the curtains. I could perhaps adopt his Oedipus, facing the fierce sphynx, adipose and oppressive.

Cautious academy, Romantic blushing? Does it all end in that back of Kiki's, *Le Violon d'Ingres*, radiant bequest from Man Ray, or has the nouveau roman rescued it, has pop art reduced it?

instant

Few things are comparable to the sun over a green meadow, to the sun over a green meadow striped with shadows, to a blue-black grackle that fluffs its feathers for a toasted-brown grackle (that is, a male for its female) and moves from the light green to the dark green, like a pawn free of the hand that plays it. Few things are comparable to the wind that moves such very distinct trees equally, drawing a gentle noise and a gentle smell toward this space that has suddenly opened up inside this immense, desiccated hovel where cars roar, and I just want to be a sound.

K

Klee

To the tune of a mythical childhood, Klee's color scale
parts the torpor of twilight like a ship. His twittering
machine opens the frontier to fertile country and the
world brightens. What will spring forth, a painting or
something else? Crystal or blood? Only everything.
The baleless arrows faithfully advance in their space.
Labyrinths pretend freedom. Cities unfurl on the
horizon. Klee's geometry is non-Euclidian. He
claims the right to be as mobile as nature. From *Blaue
Reiter* to *Blaue Vier*, his painting 'takes shape' and can
be 'Star, Vase, Plant, Animal, Head, or Man'. Never did
a happy stroke need an explanation. Klee does not
want to show man as he is but rather as he could be,
among other stars, for example. Klee – sclerosis of the
skin – dies little by little, strangely, but dances in his
paintings, in his etchings: dance of the grieving child,
dance of the moth, transformed into rhythmic trees,
the temple of longing 'thither'. In the end, when
his hand no longer responds, he will dance with the
spatula. Music has always accompanied him. Music is
his other fortune.

klērikós

I am neither a dipsomaniac nor an enologist nor a taster. I am not cultivated in matters of drinking, but I am not without a palate. I like good wine, red, certain types, and certain brands. The nose's rejections indiscreetly anticipate pretensions from the taste buds, which reject high-proof alcohols. In many countries most people seem not to know how to drink, that is, they do not know how to partake of its pleasure and instead its pleasure partakes of them. The greater the general culture, the greater the selectivity and discretion. There is a culture of wine, of beer, of whisky, of vodka, of mezcal, and no doubt of many other drinks. And there is an unculture of them all: they are not savored, but absorbed indiscriminately, the flavor barely enjoyed in a rush to ingestion: a race towards a finish that should not be implicit: inebriation, drunkenness, complete impairment legitimized by chemistry and physiology lead to irresponsibility for the person who, conquered by liquor, has been lost to reason and grace and suffers the partial death of losing self-governance. A partial death that can bring about whole death. The steering wheel in one hand and a beer can in the other, sometimes a partner resting against their shoulder and an almost singing scream wrenching pacifists from their sleep as the car careens past, the intoxicated often conclude in a curve, in the best-case scenario. In the worst, they end up killing others. Since in some countries, inspectors for drivers under the influence are not in fashion, we will never know how many of the daily accidents swarming with television camerapersons are precipitated by alcohol.

The fame of poor Noah has spanned time because of his diligence in fulfilling the divine orders to build the Ark – very demanding orders if we consider the shipyards at the time – but also because of the state of pure immodesty in which his ashamed sons discovered him in his old age. But when it was time for him to drive the ark that was under his care, Noah acted with more prudence than our many ill-fated contemporaries who zigzag through the streets of all too tolerant cities.

Back in the days of the innocent *guindado* (cherry liqueur) or the discreet *clericó* (claret cup with fruit), such concerns did not exist. *Klērikós* – in Greek, 'what is allotted by fate' – refers to the fruits scooped up or not by the small ladle used to fill the glasses. The drinks at the fingertips of today's imprudent can dispense more tragic fates.

L

Lernet-Holenia

One of the many authors in that magma of
unproductive relationships that agglomerate inside
a library, Alexander Lernet-Holenia often appeared
and disappeared among papers and books moved
from one place to another without drawing attention.
Aided by his serpentine name, pierced by a hyphen,
and my faith in the publisher that had chosen him, I
bought *Baron Bagge*, a long story, and he continued
to wait. When at long last I began leafing through
it, just about to open a gap between Hofmannsthal
and Mörike where he could hibernate among
countrymen, I read: 'He went on the nine-days'
wandering of the dead that is prescribed in myth;
he drifted toward the dreamland, rode north to the
bridge of Hór or Hār where the road to Hēl begins,
to the bridge of gold that leads into the irrevocable...'
This golden bridge (I remembered a tri-color bridge
that souls must pass over and that angels, crossing it
on horseback, will one day destroy) was the hook that
hoisted me into other airs. I advanced through this
brief masterpiece. During an innocent first reading

– a form of communication I do not reject – we do not discover the author's astute plan until he wishes us to. The tale takes us from war to death's dream with seamless subtlety. Later, I would read his novels saturated with a dreary, disproportionate veneration for army ranks, weapons, military honor, duels, and courage (but without the somber skeptic that someone like Conrad would have added) that guarantees to send a fervent chill down our spines. But none like *Baron Bagge* – concise, perfect, darker than the best of Bierce's stories, without any possibility of contact between the two authors – opened such metaphysical doors to the subject of war. Over that golden bridge I also reached an almost secret garden where other admirers of Lernet-Holenia and the Baron strolled. Those who find each other in that territory delimited by the negligence of the general public are always surprised that their almost surreptitious harvest could be a shared privilege. Readers who are incapable of being otherwise always have one book they love exclusively and that they offer, like the emblem of an order, to those they deem worthy of sharing it. How many islands might there be in that archipelago stitched together by the thread of Lernet-Holenia?[14]

---

[14] Several lustrums passed following that dazzled and stimulating reading, and several publishers in the few languages I manage kept me close to the Viennese writer. Although the world has distanced itself from the peculiar values he extolled – and he had undoubtedly already begun to realize this before his death in 1976 – his voice has not lost its reserved virtue, enveloping, able to continue illuminating us with the dark lights of those destinies hurtling towards death that he oversees. Among his many liberties (none greater than confronting the routine of repeating what one knows how to do well), he allowed himself to write a novel where the mysterious matter of shifting identities explains a series of murders within a closed group: a detective and metaphysical novel in one, something that was also

library

As a young girl sitting on the ugly sofa, if I turned my head I could see a bookcase, a small library, tributary of a larger one, and at my eye level an obscured collection with covers made of a cottony gray paper across which the *Masters of the Louvre* paraded. The flesh of Rubens' floating women was divided into emphatic lacteous zones and zones that were cause for blushing, Guardi's luminous canals overpowered the dim colors of some of Corot's skies, and the Veronese greens camouflaged themselves beneath arbitrary lights whenever they were called on to appear. I am still surprised that my value scale and the fondnesses and indifferences I constructed from such precarious versions remained intact after coming face-to-face with the originals – with the truculent and hyperbolic flesh that withdraws toward the ceilings in vast decisive spaces or somniferous knots or with the joyful levity of vegetation filled with bridges and gondolas. Since then, I have felt great devotion for the mysterious Pisanello, for Antonello da Messina, for Patinir, whose fleeting landscapes, whose mythological waters I seek out like prizes, few and far between, in corners where the greedy are not.

Lying on its side, light blue and golden, a *Summa Artis* accumulated mastabas, pyramids, pectorals, wonders in lapis lazuli and turquoise, and Nefertiti's prodigious beauty; in it I confirmed my fondness for Tutankhamun, initiated years earlier in other sources (subterranean ones: a basement that held bound volumes of *L'Illustration*) and my partiality for judging his gradual score-settling with Lord Carnarvon and

---

ventured by Leo Perutz, another admirable juggler of the inescapable, and of course by Chesterton.

company, even though we are indebted to them for so much recovered beauty. The 'letters' began at my hand level. There was, and perhaps I never delighted in it enough, an unabridged *War and Peace* in which no audacious act had mutilated Pierre's masonic initiation, in his pursuit of a *nihil obstat*. In my first readings (there were more later) I was drawn not to Natasha's lithe figure or the romance between Vera and Andrei, but to the bellicose backdrop and arabesques of strategy, which is why I am terrified whenever I think about the human being's primitive inclination for maneuvers of power and death.

Occupying a timid place beside it, Murger's *Scenes of Bohemian Life* offered me a choice between melodrama and humor. Because I am fortified with the latter, I evaded Zola's anfractuous proximity with the help of a modest imagination. Before moving on to Swift, *Penguin Island*, a work that has fallen into disuse as much as the Dreyfus affair has into oblivion, showed me irony's potential in a text of two minds, a possible way of approaching the *hypocrite lecteur* who refuses to see the reality around them. Afterwards, I was ready to follow Gulliver on his travels.

At my feet, humiliated because down there dust sought its natural serenity with greater determination, Madame de Staël's *Corinne*, Samuel Smiles (I forget what), the rosy Bernardin de Saint Pierre, and something from Carlos Reyles hated one another as they waited undeservingly for the *goel* who might free them from each other's company. Since one of the chores assigned to me – more for disciplinary reasons than domestic necessity – was to maintain order and tidiness in that little library that now nobody touched, the books were placed according to clear dietetic dispositions. Future admirations and disdains upheld those hierarchies established early on, from a literary standpoint also. Eclectic admirations, arbitrary disdains, perhaps, but spontaneous and my own. Perhaps from those few initial books I learned that a faithful relationship with them requires risking judgment, which is one more gift they give us.

Next to that space where I felt almost safe was the frontier: novels from the Nelson collection, white, gilded, French, unintelligible; and Carducci and D'Annunzio and Goldoni and others, in Italian, equally beyond my reach, regardless of how often I riffled through their pages imagining a magic moment of sudden comprehension, like with the language of the birds after biting into a particular leaf. It would not take long for me to access Goldoni thanks to the patience of Uncle Pericles, who read some of his works to me, slowly, not so much to find the exact translation but to puritanically censor it. And when French was just beginning to open its door to me, a work by Bordeaux was of great service, though maybe he was not worth all the effort: fed up with 'not being able', I read him with a dictionary and then without, in a second and immediate rereading.

If I could return to that house today, my people and things (and the house itself) having disappeared many years ago, and found by some miracle that small library with every one of those books where they once were, I do not think there is anything I would change about the order that I steadily imposed upon them, which my memory preserves and which I still hold to be sensible.

life

Hollow towering column,
life.
But close to the ground, inside
— like a dove in a dark nest —
hope.

lucidity

The despotic and foresighted king who in traditional folklore orders the destruction of all knives,
scissors, and other assorted blades in his kingdom to
impede the fatal fulfillment of a prediction — a theme
conceived earlier in mythology with Croesus and his
son Atys — must have demanded that all analytical
blades be blunted also. Only this way could he ensure
the happiness he desired for his son. For how can a
son cheerfully revel in his parents and ancestors if
he has set about judging them? How can he devote
himself openly to friendship if on various occasions he
confirmed the rarity of its fruit? It is difficult to trust
political blather after repeatedly receiving the lashings
that cause cynicism and arrogance to manifest behind
the back of justice. It is even more difficult to trust
any intelligence that tolerates intimacy with stupidity,
any honesty that allows passages through labyrinths
clouded by others. But magic knives are few and far
between, and not many people practice lethal analysis.
Today the king should leave his son in the bosom of
one of those universities that will prepare him in the
simple, lightly-marinated mold of the bien-pensants,
an effective bloodletting of all lucid thought, of all
thought. Thus, the legend's contemporary version
could achieve that rose-colored ending that parents
desire, be they kings or not.

lunacy

I

> *Man has a tropism for order. Keys in one pocket,*
> *change in another. Mandolins are tuned G D A E.*
> Nathanael West

Two after one,
three before four,
the lock on the door,
the door in place,
the minutes numbered,
the winter books,
the summer wicker,
the past in its box,
the future, awaited.

And the branch of disorder,
the trepidation in the intonation,
the commotion in the motionless,
the space in the inundated,
the pain in the laughter,
the ash in the mouth?
And suddenly the wind,
a threnody for the dead:
the future attained.

II

> *Un matto è un capolavoro inutile.*
> Giorgio Manganelli

Sometimes repaying debts becomes the dominant
concern during the end times of a person on the brink
of 'joining the majority', an encouraging way perhaps

of referring to death. Pecuniary dues are important, and it is not dishonorable to prevent a survivor from losing their confidence in someone who can no longer say anything. We acquire other debts, no less imperious, imprecise, general, and difficult to square, from voluntary benefactors who even without having had us in mind surrounded us with emotions, new ways of seeing the world, incessantly amplifying, informing, defining it. This debt never decreases no matter what we do. All the same, it is good to attempt to repay it and realize that it never expires. A debt to infinite characters, all of them real: those we knew in the flesh – their bones a pure act of our faith – and those no less real placed before us by beloved writers, those with the advantage of undeniable immortality over the former, eternal Iphigenia for her sacrificed innocence, eternal Alice in the delightful levity of her visit to the disturbing court of a hysterical queen, singular Orlando, eternal man/woman. And I'll pause here, on the precipice of an endless enumeration.

But there are also others of lesser lineage who trample one another to reach my memory together, perhaps because their heads are all slightly rising into the air. I do not resist their invasion: they have conditioned me not to ignore them. A cast of recurring characters would appear whenever my grandmother spoke, some characterized by a shared taste for flashy colors. In those days, these were reserved for costumes chosen symbolically by Carnival professionals – assorted masks, that is, individuals who wished to be an attraction on their own, clowns, cabezudos – or troupes and ensembles. She would fondly mention the 'Little Parrots of Cordón', three sisters whose last and first names were a mystery. The Little Parrots wore only green, sometimes a vibrant green like a cheery parrot, hence their designation genitively complemented with the neighborhood they brightened with their trichotomic strolls. Since there was never one without the others, we deduced that those graces each possessed their own outfit, green from their hats down to their shoes. Procuring the latter during that modest and ashen time was no simple task: it required a bespoke shoemaker able to locate leather in such an uncommon color, which led everyone interested in those women who were assumed to be unmarried to believe they were the well-to-do descendants of a good family. Their equitable advance down our main avenue, unhurried and befitting their display, seemed to take them and bring them to and from pastry shops or theaters. But no. No one ever saw them stationary in public. They preferred to be the spectacle and feed off the emotions they aroused. What they wanted was to walk, harmonious and green, in the late afternoon.

As a girl I would have liked to follow them to see what they talked about, where they lived, enter the nooks and crannies of that kitschy novel they escaped from each day. But by the time I was old enough to venture out into the world alone, all three had already disappeared; I will never know where, whether it was to a voluntary asylum or one decided by relatives who were ashamed or desirous of their green inheritance or to some other setting more in accordance with their common dream. Perhaps one of them reached the green pastures for which they were surely predestined, and her diminished sisters in mourning lost their taste for exhibition-promenades.

Other minor creatures came along to satisfy that common habit among 'normal' people of encircling an electrifying presence with insulators, measuring the distance between their behavior and that individual who is either unsuccessful or uninterested in joining the group. Some were theatrical and brought us joy. I recall the not so frequent vision of a girl dressed in discordant colors who wore socks with horizontal yellow, green, and red stripes and a similar hat. She entered a hall where a concert or a conference was about to be held. She walked down one aisle, crossed in front of the first row of seats, turned up the other aisle in the opposite direction and left, all the while rhythmically tossing a small purse in the air and flawlessly catching it. Some time later I came across her again in the street, wearing the same clothing and with the same little purse that rose and fell magnetically into her hand. But this character lacked a plot, not to mention a purpose. And she was perhaps excessively symmetrical.

Sporadic lunatics, solitaries out of their element, replace each other inside the vast spectrum that ranges from a slight clinamen of normality to absolute delirium. One day, one bearing a first and last name (legitimate or not, I do not know) arrived in various acts and roles. In some of these he proved to be a plagiarist, introducing an unusual nuance into this human comedy.

He went by Arenales something, they said, without a proper name. Maybe he had a family. Under the cloak of madness, a black one, he donned a black suit and black cravat. And he wore, always, a black broad-brimmed slouch hat, very nineteenth century. His insanity was attuned to the seasons and this was his winter uniform. In summer's 38 degrees he sported a Palm Beach, a light-colored suit made with lightweight fabric, and paradoxical gaiters, also light-colored and very insulating.

He often walked past my house, near the university whose auditorium hosted weekly events. There I heard concerts and Neutra, Neruda, Duhamel, León Felipe, and many others. There Vaz Ferreira delivered his incisive lessons before a handful of people. Standing at one of the side doors, Arenales would look with disdain at the day's guest and the audience in the parterre. He made clear his disagreement with everyone from that uncomfortable but visible position, leaning against the handrail of the stairs that lead up the tiers. From his pocket emerged a newspaper that he would open up to immerse himself in its reading, making as much noise as he possibly could. Every now and then he would resurface and cast an inclement glance at the world, which made no reaction. He had resolved the predicament that his hat presented when handling the newspaper by leaving it atop his head, even though back then men respected the convention that they should remove it indoors. Perhaps he held a libertarian perspective on that matter and wished to mortify those who distractedly looked at him to see if he was still there. I was intrigued when I saw him, the first time. Later I learned to tolerate him, as something ugly and preexistent, like other aspects of the hall's decor.

I was attending law school at that point. Giribaldi Oddo was teaching first-year criminal law, and his appearance conveyed what we all knew, that he was sick. On top of that, the subject was no laughing matter and a sepulchral silence reigned throughout. The days were beautiful, an autumn that was still warm. One morning shortly after class had begun, the door opened. We all looked over slightly startled, given the professor's sensitivity to tardiness and interruptions. Framed by the outside light, we saw Arenales' eccentric silhouette still in his summer garb, light-colored and with gaiters, his sparse, gray mane disheveled by the breeze from the open cloister on the upper floor. He demonstrated he was aware that a class was not a lecture open to the public when he uttered with composed submissiveness: 'Are questions allowed?' to which Giribaldi, who had perhaps never had a sense of humor even on his best days, looking at him like a stone about to fall, responded with a 'No' so deep and terminal that Arenales took one step back and closed the door, defeated but discreet.

He made one final appearance in my life. While I was buying something in a small neighborhood haberdashery, the young employee, clearly a student, asked pointing behind me: 'Do you know him? Is that really Sábat Ercasty?' Sábat Ercasty had been our literature professor and was the father of one of my classmates since school whom I cherished greatly along with her mother Tula and him; I owed them my first invitation to the circus and often went to their house. I turned around: out in the street Arenales was walking by, and I laughed at the confusion. 'I ask because he came in here and gave that name.' I realized then that his black attire and his hat was in imitation of Sábat. Even the cravat, which a younger Tula had tried to replace with a less poetic tie. I doubt he would have been pleased with this usurpation of his personality. I never mentioned it to him.

The black suit transports me to another character, whom it is perhaps unfair of me to include here. But he seems to want to show his face. He was the brother of Rafael Barradas, the painter who left us magnificent works like his unforgettable portraits of blue-eyed angels that rival those by Modigliani. A friend of Lorca and Dalí, he was a regular illustrator for *Alfar*, the magazine we shared with the Spaniards. (Julio J. Casal was as Montevidean as the Rambla, and his magazine, founded in Spain, was one of the best and longest running we ever had, though controversial for its generosity.)

This brother of his used to sit alone in cafés with an ever-present packet wrapped with several loops of string. A book or a notebook? He aspired to be a famous writer without owing anything to Barradas. Because he thought Pérez, his first last name, was insufficiently noble and distinguishable to grace the cover of the masterpiece he had written or would write, he took to calling himself Antonio de Ignacios. Dressed in a close-fitting black suit with a flat-brimmed Cordovan hat, they called him 'Barradas's widow'. You felt the urge to sound a party horn in his face, mostly covered by his slightly greasy, bohemian-writer black locks. I was never able to find out anything concrete (comical or tragic) about him nor get a sense of the mysterious content in that bundle to know whether the truths it contained were sane or mad. He published two less-than-mediocre books that included verses, texts in prose, and brevities – I dare not call them *greguerías* – that, despite their barbarism, betrayed a reading of the great Ramón.

We all know that lunacy's subtle rainbow ranges from pale to intense. I have forgotten much of the first sort, but I always remember that Tomás Segovia, having once lived in Montevideo and drawn his own conclusions, used to say that it reminded him of London because of a similar obsession with drinking tea (and at five o'clock), which in Mexico is reserved for times of illness, and because it is filled with eccentrics.

But since not everything ends 'in Montevideo, where everything always begins', Enrique Fierro *dixit*, I will close this letter with an impeccable image, as if enveloped by clouds, that frequently brightened my Austinite streets, generally so rational: a beautiful, flawless woman between forty and fifty who moved about this city, which today is still somewhat removed from formality but was even more small-town back then, dressed in clothing that looked like it came straight from the wardrobe of a theater a few days before opening night, always distinct, always of the period (though I could not say which). The first time I saw her, in a small market, I was not so surprised by her costume that included a birch broom and a floral crown. She was with a matching companion. I pictured them enlivening a school festival by heralding the arrival of spring. After that I always saw her on her own. The last time, the most indelible, wrapped in a light-blue shawl, she recreated the traditional image of the Virgin Mary, as if ready to depart for heaven. Perhaps she had been forewarned by some angel because her touch of fantasy never again crossed my humdrum paths.

M

mamboretá

My pedagogical family, consisting mostly of unmarried adults of both sexes, initiated me at an early age in the contemplation of the evil of the world. Instead of the dog I was never allowed to have and before the rabbit with whom they pressured me into an impossible bilateral relationship, to comfort me they captured a praying mantis. I learned later that most people in Río de la Plata call it a *mamboretá*, with its beautiful Guarani drum roll.

They successfully kept me in an almost hypnotic state for long stretches of time beside the jar that confined it. That little creature seemed fashioned from an elongated emerald. Its charms were few: its color and spindly shape, which allowed it to disguise itself among the twigs with which I attempted to recreate a welcoming habitat, the cunning movements of its legs equipped with fine saws, and that head with eyes that looked on impassively, positioned askew along the green stem of its body. Its way of eating the flies that I, somewhat disgusted, trapped and presented to it as I had been instructed, was not something I

125

was ever able to find attractive. It was apparent that when my clumsiness delivered them dead, its enthusiasm was limited, but if they were within its grasp and alive, it hunted and ate them with delectation, starting at the head with an enthusiastic malignance that was not without elegance in the maneuvering of its legs, in its entire posture. It was like witnessing an act of anthropophagy with a knife and fork. It had company, perhaps so that I could complete my observations. There must be a time of year when mantises thrive. Uncle Pericles devoted part of his considerable leisure time to hunting another specimen from the garden. To his dismay, it turned out to be male. We soon learned that the first one was female. After a brief period of friendship, during which my Clytemnestra hid her awful customs from her partner, the male succumbed to her allure. I was not present for the hymeneal occasion because it was not yet time for me to be initiated into certain mysteries. I arrived late, for dessert. The lack of explanations concerning the missed beginning of the ceremony led me to believe that it consisted entirely in the consort's disappearance inside an astonishingly capable female. I understood the utility of that jagged saw by the speed of the carving and the reason for the peculiar configuration of her head, her jaws oriented for maximum efficacy. Now I only needed to establish the relationship, which might have been obvious had I been more mistakenly astute, between the matrimonial customs of that fleeting couple and the (perhaps defensive) bachelorhood of my untamed uncles.

memory

A wax tablet, undoubtedly murky and small and not with the proper consistency, according to Plato. According to Pliny, our most fragile part. But what is certain is that when someone is willing to sink into that lesser agony of discouragement, it offers the transmission of distant fires that warm the place where it might grow wings. And when the need arises to hibernate for a few moments, to seek a maternal cave in which to invoke repair, it offers an ekphrasis, a bright detachable fragment, a skein of successive epiphanies, liquidambar trees at whose feet, hearkening back to earlier times, we regain our strength. It can thus be indulgent, pleasant, soothing. Also, it is sometimes to blame when the shrewdest of the wild animals coils itself about the tree and suggests it can be utilized in a rapacious revision of power. Torment will ensue, the treachery that promptly offers you, after twice that, nothing.

model

The perfect composition, the grace of movement, the singing colors, and, in many cases, the beauty of the portrayed face tend to erase any thought of the patient model's benumbed calvary, so infrequently spared from forced positions. We are touched by the love that Saskia's image emits in the paintings of Rembrandt (though the painter's own image is no less obsessive, slipping his self-portrait beneath helmets and feathers, in varied disguises inspired by the Bible or seraglios), or the image of Cranach the Elder's familiar model or Vermeer's. (Should I again mention Kiki's back-*Violon d'Ingres*? But photographs, like this one from Man Ray, are faster and therefore more compassionate to those posing in the nude.) The love exuded and the undeniable art make us forget about the hours of mandatory stillness imposed upon the feminine collaborator, in this case consisting of docility and a serene spirit, the hidden history on the dense reverse side of the visible image.

On the other hand, when looking at still lifes or *natures mortes*, we imagine the painter alone in the fight against putrefaction, a sign of times prior to artificial and preservative cold. Despite their apparently problem-free repose, fish, hares, partridges, ducks, or pheasants, beneath their scales, skins, or feathers in colors and seductive shades, avenge the living and submissive models by forcing the painter to hurry, something the most patient sitter, a less tolerant king, noble, or cardinal, or the most insufferable lady would not do. Corruption lies in wait for the subject matter, ready to transform appearances and offend the nose regardless how suited the latter may have been to the aggressions that previous centuries considered normal, even the one belonging to the artist absorbed in the pursuit of the lines their hand produces in response to the acuity of their sight. Slowness, along with the warmth the painter no doubt needs to avoid going numb during their sedentary task, can be fatal for the perishable shape that is their inspiration. Thoughts originating in decomposition can disturb the peace of their spirit, the creator's necessary belief in permanence. Do we not have to keep the idea of death at bay, the idea of being perishable that clings to almost everything, in order to resist the temptation to do nothing and be able to engage in that struggle against difficulty and discouragement that is creation?

monologue

I

Of the dwarf: 'Is it possible that such a flood might overtake me now? Will these miserable hills made of mud and inhabited by blond men spit down on me, on me who has contended with the heights of my country? On me who descends from viceroys, who can trace my ancestry back, way back, who redresses and dresses my history and everyone else's and collects and does not pay, exacting exactor, could I not confine them all to secret dungeons? I would summon them to the ship's brig. Oh, glory of medieval punishments: a rooster and a monkey (another), a dog and a snake (another, another) together in a barrel with the convict of a serious crime. What could be more fitting for the trouble-maker? That maximum and centrifugal sentence; cast far he who has dared challenge my worldly experience. I, multiparous and omnivore, in tit for tat decreed submission or targe, orthodoxy or orthopedics for the insolent. Has the Iscariot not understood our *modus vivendi*?

'Nugatory am I, nugatory are we, my dignitary and I, my *ne plus ultra*, my easily agitated, my *Amanita phalloides*. Sometimes, it is true, I vilify him in the presence of whoever is on hand because his hands touch where they should not, and I find out. I know you fear me, you cannot hide it since, as you must have heard, I am a witch. When I bite, I know what the one bitten is thinking; I scheme and I know what the one embroiled is thinking; and when I give and take, I know what I am losing. Raise your testudos to defend yourselves from my projectile tongue, raise them, because I no longer care if I lose the kingdom. Other people imparadise, I risk imprisonment, I vomit, anastrophe of the world's order. And yet, sometimes I would like, oh *quidam*, ambulatory *quid pro quo*, oh perplexing question, to truly be that person my heuristic invents, that person I conceive so I can see if the world believes me, conceives me again, truly, not falsely, with lies and poison.'

II

Of the thief: 'I am an assiduous ant, unrivaled in my affability with my future victim and even with those past. I never lose anything, not even my charm. Exuding joy when I see you, I care for my clientele because what greater assurance that I can steal from you than having already stolen from you? Pursuing fatty and even succulent portions, I go slowly until the time comes to go quickly. Nothing weighs too heavy for my home and so, since the profession I prefer most is that of representative and I also have a strong fondness for letters of all types, I will take books unless letters of credit fall into my clutches. Even works of art work for me, and if the painters are dead, so much the better because we who are artful know that their contribution to our clandestine financial aid is more valuable.

'A man so silent in his actions does well – though it could carry certain legal risks – to have a wife who sings. And I had one. Perhaps not everything fits in the musical scale. Perhaps not reasoning. In this, then, I was an agile discobolus, showering her with the discs that expand in my hands through my impervious purloining. She might be the same in her own way, allowing my soul and, if I succeed, my soft and pedagogical hands too, the opportunity to venture into youthful fields. But those are other offenses and a different circle.

'It matters not; in the meantime, I will reign in silence, trusting that other services and a certain amount of sympathy will, in the long run, cause my victims to abandon their initial and legitimate objective of canceling me, more that I actually am, with the retribution I deserve. I could not fault them, since the work began more than half a century ago by my blessed and irrefutable mother who did so much to transform me into this person of tightfisted subterfuges that I have been throughout my entire phantasmal life.'

III

Of a polygon: 'I suffer from anamorphosis, I have one face and another and another. And do not look for me where I no longer am because though I am a companion to all and an accomplice in whatever, I compare and come forward only if it is convenient and not where I was previously lingering. I am the contrary of nothingness: nothingness *nomine est et re non est* and I am something, but I have no name.

'I maybe take unfair advantage of mirrors, always at the service of my variable surface. I am like the hyena, according to Brunetto Latini, sometimes male, sometimes female, but out of mere fickleness, whatever tickles my fancy, colorless or yellow, with black markings: a mapepire.[15] While I am careful not to drink because *in vino veritas*, I do walk sigmoidally, which ultimately takes me where I had not previously planned to be.

'Someone can attempt to identify me. There is no sense in trying. Society has become accustomed to me – to those who are like me – and they cover me

---

[15] A Venezuelan viper, venomous and aggressive.

with a cloak of cheap concealment. Perhaps today my way of being is in their best interest, to see the morass in which I protect myself grow larger: someone must be in charge of igniting confusion, of fanning the flames, of calling things by the wrong name. In short, I am the constant arrow that hits the target of the disaster on the horizon, the door, seemingly the way out, that is always closed.'

Montevideo (the Other)

> Lançar as barcas ao Mar–
> De névoa, em rumo de incerto...
> –Pra mim o longe é mais perto
> Do que o presente lugar.
> Mário de Sá-Carneiro

I have subjected myself for years, out of love for Montevideo, to the creation of a magical and tempestuous city, established amidst waters and winds, that could very well share that same strange, invented, contentious name: Montevideo. That is, *Monte VI de E. a O.*, Hill 6 from East to West.

Names that designate cities also receive an enveloping aura in return. The sonority of a few theurgic syllables sends particles of what it names into the air and forever affixes them to the most receptive of all substances, to the memory of those who detest 'reality's tedious game'. This is the case for me with Basra, Uppsala, Urgell, and, for some, Montevideo. The world is offended by duplications it considers useless, and we who have fallen into that sin of supposed wastefulness withdraw, taking our perverse but innocent imaginations to places of greater shade.

My Montevideo, like Cartagena de Indias, is surrounded by previsionary pink and gray stone walls whose primary task is to prevent the scent of orange blossom, honeysuckle, and eucalyptus from escaping and the invasion of marine odors from becoming too tumultuous. Within, this fragrant summation courses through the impeccable, tree-lined streets with invariant, sensible names paying recognized and accepted homages. The names are beautiful, sometimes because they are Guarani, sometimes because they are old, but their beauty is always respected and transmitted from one century to the next. The colors of the city vary, 'between yellow or green or date-colored', according to the seasons or the readers, according to the ash trees, the ginkgoes, the sycamores, or the chinaberries.

Who in their works, even imaginary ones, does not guard certain preferences? In this one of mine, so arduous and incomplete that I must look after it every second or it will collapse, I insist on constructing the adjacent sea. To watch how it sprawls and selects its shades, I have to turn my back to the city. At times it is entirely undertow, although that sea is not imaginary but rather false, perhaps the only false thing in this real imaginary city. This is of little consequence; neither the gulls nor the dolphins seem to care, and they make use of its estuary waters as if they were those of the most nomadic and irrefutable sea.

All the same, a real-life esplanade runs alongside it and each day, at a certain point, simultaneous abyss and summit begin, rapt stillness and atomic vertigo, the city's most legitimate and eternal conquests: 'the four ardent sculptures: Lautréamont, Laforgue, Herrera y Reissig, Agustini'.

Those four imaginary statues, embracing in radiant camaraderie atop the lofty, truly real territory of the spirit, that Neruda saw shaking each other's 'dark-stone hands' on the shores of reality, now exist. And not only in the Chilean's words; also in the conviction of a Mexican, J. E. Pacheco, convinced he had walked around them one drunken sunset. And in the feelings of a character from the Cuban-Mexican novelist Julieta Campos who 'with softened eyes caresses the statue of Lautréamont on Montevideo's esplanade as if it were his property'.

But there is another false city, changed by outrage, that reflects the same sea, abominable repeater, a city where anger and empty words arose, where that plaza of distortion opened up like a chasm, which for one poet functions as a cupel of embers in non-imaginary places. No monument in this city has been worthy of testifying to the true existence of a myth, none have been celebrated like those in the other, the authentic one.

There is also a hospital, 'the great Hospital of Montevideo, with its large chandeliers hanging from the ceiling and many delirious men in their beds and an incredibly beautiful Spanish nun...' The shape that corresponds to this reconstruction, made with the same concrete we all transit, is, I believe, Hospital Maciel, near the port. It was no doubt there where Hugo von Hofmannsthal, afflicted with some malady, docked during one of his periodic pilgrimages in search of the implicit truth in the life of men, which he wanted to read on their faces as one might read a hieroglyphic, a sign. There he forever heard a young Englishman in a neighboring bed, who would die a year later, speak a phrase that the latter had heard from his father: *The whole man must move at once.*[16]

The Viennese writer would never forget this phrase, transformed into one of his foundational truths, that appears in his *Book of Friends*. In 1901, at the end of this period of transhumance, he returned to Austria and like anyone who has intensely experienced the particularities of elsewhere, he felt lost among the things of his homeland and wrote in *Letters of the Traveler Who Returned* how in Montevideo, at that time, he had encountered upstanding creatures with their grand patriarchal demeanor that was, in his words, nostalgic. Hofmannsthal, who was capable of searching the earth for that essence fallen into disuse, harmony, was another of those who helped build that image every city needs to be truly alive and free of the danger of extinction.

An image that can be fleeting and suspended in the sky, like the one the ill-fated Italian poet Dino Campana gave us when, among the dunes, from the ship that was taking him to Buenos Aires, 'the coastal capital appears above a sea yellow with the magnificent bounty of the river, of the new continent. The evening light limpid, cool, and electric…' The light in Montevideo that is real and fabulous.

Floating above the city's logical, monotonous, colonially gridded architecture – because Bruno Mauricio de Zabala did not design Montevideo in circles, like Campanella did his City of the Sun – is a rambling plane with its undulations and its curves and its meandering and unevenness where the imaginative, given over to wonderment, would like to lose themselves. All who love the city place their desires,

---

[16] Georg Christoph Lichtenberg took this same phrase from the same place, Addison's *The Spectator*, as the motto for one of his provocative and inexhaustible journals of notes and aphorisms.

their dreams in this sky, remove or raise walls, colors, perspectives, gardens, rescue hidden trees, banish the people who crucify them. Every morning, afternoon, or night well spent in the created city adds a definite corner to the other one, dubious and unstable, the one that dwindles little by little.

A city is a language with its different levels. There is a language that is profound and, for that reason, secret and not transmittable from one being to another, performed only between the metropolis and each of them. And so in reality there are as many languages as there are inhabitants. Then there is the other language, superficial, which as such is best expressed on a surface, on walls. The two cities again come face to face. The legitimate one was intuited, once more, by Neruda, who read on its 'walls the word poetry'. Perhaps someday we will discover that poetry is circulating in secret. The false one imposes its graffiti on all of us with the immodest despotism of its wit, sometimes original, or with its diverse, ruinous, and no less authoritarian propaganda.

Morandi, Giorgio

I

INCURSION INTO THE PALAZZO D'ACCURSIO. Here the Armadillo takes five minutes to rest. Rest for this absurd but charming machine imitating the woodwork, bronze, and glass of an old-fashioned trolley car but with a motor that supplies the electricity from which it has been liberated? For the driver, more likely, and for the passenger who endures the lurches of this dinosaur that Austin nurtures and reproduces as one of its distinctive features. The low wall that surrounds the campus where we stand waiting is another.

Its stones come from an area that was once submerged and offer infinite molds of fossilized shells. On the wall's edge, someone has left a half-eaten apple, the familiar soda can, and another empty container. I envision a still life and consider the distance separating this mixture of objects from those portrayed in paintings and with little need to dignify them (only be at their level): fruits, animals, flowers, a glass bottle, a shape. I am not thinking of pop art. I could. Or I could think of Velázquez, or Cézanne. But the lesson of Morandi is all too fresh in my mind.

Giorgio Morandi was born, lived, and died in Bologna, Italy. My memory of the city was subdued, the fault of the chicken coops and the kitchens, the breastfeeding babies and their mothers, the noble attitudes of members of diverse professions that I had encountered, decades earlier, in an enormous and stale exhibition of nineteenth-century Bolognese painting. Its emanations saturated and effaced everything else. Discovering that I had been unfair with the city was a pleasant complement to the wonder of an almost complete collection of Morandi.

The Palazzo d'Accursio, from the twelfth century, on one side of the Piazza Maggiore, houses the communal art collections. Another wing was dedicated to Morandi, adapting it to the simplicity that he would have liked. Many of the world's great museums have an example of his work, one of his still lifes. Whoever has stood before one of them could recognize the painter; whoever has been won over with a single work by Morandi is no superficial sampler of paintings. It would then be difficult for them to be satisfied with such scant information. Today Bologna's painter is its greatest attraction. Its halls were filled with successive donations, primarily from his sisters Anna, Dina, and Maria Teresa. In 1961, following the reorganization of the Gallery of Modern Art, Giorgio himself anonymously donated a *natura morta* of his own, three years before he died, blending a sense of humor and confidence in his work. Later, the sisters ceded his personal collection of paintings and engravings from other periods, its greatest virtue being its testament to the artist's respect for a past that one might assume was, for him, remote.

The painter's whole life can be found in those halls, that is, almost his whole life, his first sketches, his early academic works, his mature oil paintings, his etchings, his drawings, his late watercolors. His thematic field is brief: a few portraits, a few landscapes, and then objects, reiteratively, variations on a softly modulated piece of music, 'memory's objects' that occupy the largest space in his work and reappear time and time again, recorded in one or another of his preferred techniques. They make up the museum like they made up Morandi's creative trajectory. Inside the exhibition, an exact reproduction of his workshop awaits the public, and at the entrance we are welcomed by glass cases displaying his models, no doubt collected one by one from lowly antique shops: unassuming things chosen for their shape, their texture, for who knows what mysterious response to the painter's sensibility. For anyone familiar with Morandi's work, these are as identifiable as Saskia's face is for those familiar with Rembrandt.

There is no painter, I believe, who has extracted so much plastic abundance from a limited group of objects, achieving such powerful distinction as to impose himself iconically with an empire like the one derived from the human face, even the highly statuary one of the primitives. Roberto Longhi, the art historian who wrote *Breve ma veridica storia della pittura italiana* when he was twenty-four years old and who would form a close relationship with Morandi, bases his own discovery of 'the diagonal of the cube' in Caravaggio on the Cézannean principle of approaching nature via the cylinder, the sphere, and the cone. Morandi applies the same principle to his landscapes, but most of all to the objects that more immediately materialize (I was going to say 'incarnate') their shapes. The 'lyricism' that so greatly concerned Longhi appears in Morandi's color agreements: Cesare Garboli identifies one of Longhi's texts on Piero della Francesca, from 1914, that seems to describe Morandi's much later works: 'pale pink and autumnal violet approach a powerful shade containing red and light and dark browns'. It is not unusual that the person who ignored Braque and Picasso and mocked Surrealism and de Chirico's 'orthopedic gods' was, with his sway as an international critic, the first to identify the exceptional nature of the Bolognese's work to his astonished fellow citizens. (In 1930, a guidebook of local art still chose to ignore him, and there were some critics who reproached his return to the past, to Cézanne, to Chardin, to Pompeii…) Longhi was an undeniable supporter of the solitary painter when, despite the brevity of the latter's early Futurist adventure (how could his still organisms, deep and introspective, ever interact with the velocity that Marinetti required?), the former seemed to leave him in one strand of pictorial trends in the experiments of the avant-garde.

If the centuries were to erase Morandi's name from his works, as they have with so many painters in the past, he would remain more than any other contemporary as 'the painter of *natura morta*'. But this title would need to be corrected, its terminology inappropriate in his case: it would be better to speak of *still life*. Objects, not nature, more typically fill his works, and they are endowed with the most surprising life. Even his flowers usually have cloth or paper models. In his studio – itself a still life, preserved in its colors and in the already plastic arrangement of its every element – one of his vases holding a dried bouquet, revived in painting in pale pink and 'autumnal violet' (veering the slightest bit from ivory, the key for almost all his visual music), recalls his singular struggle to govern the work before it is formulated.

Not only did he try to preserve his personal freedom inside a city, inside his family – his sisters – by making that minute room-workshop the center of his world; for nature to be accepted by him, it also had to yield to his rules, exchange its own vibrations for those he prescribed. He had his landscapes close at hand in Grizzana, his country house later in life, or in the small Bolognese parks: Villa Margherita, or Montagnola across the way, or, even closer, the Cortile di Via Fondazza, the open space behind his house. One version of it, the one from 1958, is remarkable for the synthesis and relationship of its volumes and for the persuasiveness of the contrast that appears between the sky's lilac gray, the salmon pinks of some walls and roofs and the cream color of others against two vertical fields and several dark brown patches. From this confrontation emerges an intense, unforgettable presence of sun and summer, that is, of the outside world.

The composition correlates the light-colored parallels that cross the sky with two dark brown horizontals near the houses and a nest of television antennas, symmetrical to the light lines that hint at windows. I have stood before this often-reproduced work to determine its contrast with 'memory's objects' where there is no summer but rather an inner season that maintains shades of a perpetual autumn, the painter's *mental season*, one could say.

In his paintings of objects as well as his landscapes, Morandi complies with Diderot's demand: *Peindre comme on parlait à Sparte.*[17] The writer, who upon seeing Boucher's paintings exclaimed: *Toutes ses compositions font un tapage insupportable,*[18] would have been satisfied with the silence that flows from the space in which Morandi's models are recorded, that space always held by the inevitable angle of two planes and two tones.

While Italy suffered the upheavals that the twentieth century – like every century – abundantly provided, and ones which the painter was not always able to escape, inside his tiny dominion he ignored the passage of the time of accidents in the heroic search for essential time. The objects were slowly covered in dust, like people are slowly covered in wrinkles, and he painted them day after day, creating relationships between them. His studio still has that narrow table covered in paper decorated with the strokes that established exact positions for the new relationships between his models. He searched, guided by his intuition: 'All is mystery, and us, the simplest, the most insignificant of things.'

Only once, apparently by commission, did he make room in an elongated oil painting for three shapes that were unusual for him: a violin, a mandolin

---

[17] Paint as they spoke in Sparta.
[18] All his compositions make an unbearable racket.

(or bandolin), and a cornet. His frequent guests are bottles, jars, small circular or rectangular boxes, clay pottery, old coffee pots, pitchers, curious spheres that suggest the segments of an orange, whole or divided. On the walls, the brims of two felt hats without their crowns perhaps represented humble versions of an ellipse.

That obsessive, almost ritual, penetration into an essence emanating from things, that gaze that pushes aside exterior precisions in order to construct the definitive *image* around an 'optical illusion', finds a parallel in the poetic attitude of Ungaretti. When discussing his own texts in *Il deserto e dopo* (The Desert and After), he states: '*on ne peut se représenter les choses poétiquement, c'est-à-dire qu'on ne peut les saisir dans leur réalité la plus profonde que quand elles n'existent pas; et c'est à ce moment-là seulement qu'elles sont à nous, et cela par notre inspiration…*'[19] For Morandi's models, such 'no longer existing' was realized through gradual oxidation, when, slightly moved by the painter's hand, they abandoned their consumed self and reincarnated in another possibility granted by a new composition. '*Cette concentration dans l'instant d'un objet était démesurée. L'éternité éblouissait l'instant. Je ne connaitrai plus autant de sujétion, ni cette liberté, la véritable, d'un miroir constant. L'objet s'élevait aux proportions d'une figure divine. J'ai enfin compris pourquoi le Nègre fait avec des débris de miroir les yeux de son idole.*'[20]

---

[19] 'It is not possible to represent things poetically, that is to say they cannot be seized in their profoundest reality except for when they no longer exist; and only in that moment do they belong to us and that is thanks to our inspiration…' Interview with Denis Roche in *L'Herne*, Paris, 1969.

[20] 'This concentration inside the instant of an object was excessive. The instant was dazzled by eternity. I will never know so much

I am not sure if it is perhaps too bold to say that on a very intimate, very essential level, after the technical perfection of his etchings, Morandi achieves that freedom where the object reaches something similar to eternity in his final watercolors. Here, substance and shapes become leaner and reduced to incredible concentration, freed even of the space that holds them.

In Morandi's later Bolognese museum, it would not have been difficult to surround him with certain paintings coming from various parts of the world – by de Staël, Burri, Gnoli, Amalia Nieto – to show that his silence had, in the end, produced echoes.

II

THE CARACAS MORANDIS. Coincidences, which sometimes assist us, granted me another encounter with Morandi, this time unexpected. At a lunch organized by the Consolidado Cultural Foundation, sponsor of the Pérez Bonalde Prize, I had the good fortune of being seated next to the director of their collection of paintings. She was Italian and it seemed natural to tell her about my fascinating visit to the museum at the Accursio. She very kindly asked if I wanted to see the Caracas Morandis. No one had ever mentioned the Caracas Morandis to me before and I thought I had visited everything visitable during my previous visits. 'And lots of them,' she clarified.

The ignorance that had kept his paintings absent from so many museums for years made it even more

---

constraint, nor that freedom, the genuine kind, of a constant mirror. The object was elevated to the proportions of a divine body. At last, I have understood why the African makes the eyes of their idol with shards of mirror.' Ungaretti, 'Innocence et mémoire,' *La Nouvelle Revue Française*, 1926.

remarkable that about thirty works were present there in an enclave among cypress trees, totally foreign to the Caraquenian landscape, on the Cota Mil (Elevation One Thousand), the highway that circulates at that altitude. There, Señora Beatriz Arismendi de Plaza houses the collection curated by her and her husband.[21] It is not a Morandi museum: it is a very elegant selection of drawings, watercolors, oil paintings, governed by exceptional taste, its common thread. By including Ben Nicholson, Klee, Bissier, Braque, Giacometti, Picasso, Geneviève Asse, artists whom he admired or who admired him, by placing a small painting from the eighteenth century with small boxes in a small room, it favors a line of creation.

Alongside expensive works, there are beautiful bottles of different colors collected on a table. Everything creates a harmonic and thoughtful environment where commercial value is not taken into account and where each element seems to lead us by the hand to a Morandi, genuflect, and leave us on our own. As we stand in front of a Corot, a painter he greatly admired, the woman recalls her shock at the price a gallery had placed on a Morandi: 'Then how much would they ask for a Corot?'

With the triumph of Franco, Ambassador Plaza renounced his position in Spain, and they went to live in Italy where they began to follow each stage of the Bolognese's work and were able to enter his sequestered life. Above the headboard of her bed, she has one of his rare landscapes, exquisite, a gift from the painter's sisters on his death and on his behalf. We walk around, trying to visit everything, to do the impossible: store each piece of this admirable heritage

---

[21]   She has since died, and they tell me the collection is no longer in Venezuela.

in our memory. Yet another room contains a wall of first editions – Lope de Vega, Góngora, Cervantes, Ariosto, etc. – bound by artists. She remarks: 'This is actually the most valuable part of the house.'

Now in the doorway, beside her and on the checkered floor, taking one last look at the Etruscan piece I thought was a Giacometti, I can only say: 'How grateful everyone here must be to you!' I imagine her bathed in the country's veneration, considering the generosity involved in bringing this wonder and preserving it. She did not say how difficult it has to be to care for it in this climate, but she did mention what it costs her to maintain or replace the cedars and cypresses that give her 'villa' and the surrounding garden this deliberate Florentine air.

She is a widow now, without children. Lowering her beautiful gray head somewhat melancholically and ending her sentence with a long ellipsis, she responds: 'I once tried to donate it and they would not accept it...'

Morlach

Morlach (1) refers, of course, to a native of Morlachia, and Morlachia is that country on the eastern shore of the Adriatic whose dubious name was pronounced by flamboyant soldiers who at one time conspired in plays and operettas to transform European history into a collection of music, colors, and ridiculous situations.

Morlach (2) is also, in Spanish, a person who feigns foolishness and ignorance; and, in Lunfardo, it is a Spanish dollar, a piece of eight. This acceptation, solvent, is slipping away. But since I was born and lived receptively in the Río de la Plata, breathing in certain inevitable essences with the eucalyptic and marine air, 'morlacos del otario' (chump change) precipitate from Gardel's slushy voice. And since even the Royal Spanish Academy Dictionary now knows that 'otario' means 'dumb, naïve, easily deceived', how can I not feel that this polysemic 'morlach' is magnetized for rare condensations, that fate has eternally positioned it in front of a surprising mirror: the one the legitimate fool loans to the fool who merely feigns his foolishness.

move

Comme les exécutions capitales, les déménagements ont lieu à l'aube.[22] A novel by Jean-Luc Benoziglio begins with a catastrophic move, and the violence of the comparison that introduces it took me back to a distant past, to my first exercise in that agonizing task, even if it did not occur at dawn. Once it was over, it was like an incomprehensible whiplash, and I suspect it gave me a permanent feeling of insecurity: they were taking the ground from beneath my feet, the polished floors, the three patios, the lustrous oak staircase that led up to Aunt Ida's posthumous bedroom – in those days deaths were often followed by an immediate move – the little garden, and, no less important, the wallpapered walls, thresholds to a magical forest where little fairies came and went, able to sing their crossings using the wind and the espagnolette of a window, as well as the occasional malevolent goblin who had to be neutralized or defeated. I was losing the frosted-glass doors and the green, white, and orange-paned picture window that

---

[22]   Like executions, moves take place at dawn.

opened onto the patio covered with grapevines. I thought it impossible to live without all that. And they were taking away the basement and the rooftop terrace, which meant taking away future possessions to which I had always expected to have free access.

The notice with which they informed me in advance of the move made it more unbelievable. When we are young, we usually do not have a good understanding of time spans: two years was something too loose and difficult to conceive. Childhood inviscerates the steadfastness of cycles, the permanence of objects, the routine of small events, the reiteration of an appointment with times, things, people, rhythms that cannot fail without the world collapsing. Games usually have a fixed setting, though that fixity may give rise to infinite transformations. But it is essential that two armchairs maintain a constant relationship between each other and the wall, for example, so that the corner can be a grotto, the cave of some terrifying animal, a gnome's kingdom, a doll's room, a hideout where one can be invisible. Despite everything, one day the day of the transplant came, preceded by the false comedy of a week of upheaval. 'What a surprise!' my grandmother would say, annoyed to always find me where I was most in the way, somewhere on the floor in between crates filled with accommodating straw and objects that to me seemed – and some were – magnificent, brought down from a shelf that was normally beyond my reach or momentarily removed from their habitual confinement. While I amused myself imagining future parties around a tea set taken out of its storage, they were also packing up the impalpable structure of my own brief life. Like a befuddled trilby emerging from among the dust balls that had enveloped it, disoriented by so much distraction, I saw myself in the new house, still unaware that I would never like it. And to think that there are people who adore moving. I know of one person not too advanced in age who had recorded more than thirty relocations, which amounted to a new house every two years… I read somewhere that demons are unable to walk backwards. Why would they want to? When we leave something, we would be better off not returning to it. Whether backwards or forwards, it will always be with the melancholy of what is irreversible.

museum

That publicly sociable friend loved music. I often spotted him at concerts looking nervous, polite, and uncomfortable during the intermissions. He was filled with anxiety during those ten or fifteen minutes when he was usually met with as many conversation propositions as friends, some of them incompatible. The obligatory superficiality that arose from speaking to various people at once was equivalent to the difficult task of not speaking to anyone. If he managed to step away with one person, verging on a less grating and vacuous form of communication than those repeated greetings, a litany of oral symbols vague in scope, his choice could offend those excluded and the thought of that spoiled the possible conversation.

I remember that friend in museums. There one can experience a similar worry. While we are captivated standing before each work of art, a vertiginous relationship is born and grows, and it dies or deteriorates when we tear ourselves away toward another that, in turn, paralyzes and binds us for a short time to its electric space. 'The common air that bathes the globe', which Whitman spoke of, performs an equalizing function and is thus the enemy of every singular wonder, because each work is a precious moment of solitary eternity, a mystery that in order to be unlocked demands the gaze come from an eye empty of other images.

And yet, besides those frenzied and denigrated exclusive adorers of the Gioconda or the more imaginative ones of the Venus de Milo, rarely do museumgoers limit themselves to a single work, unless they are specialists. Monogamous lovers of one painting or one sculpture are, I think, nonexistent.

music

One day music appeared. Could I have thought: May God protect me? He did, and that happiness, one of the few we surrender ourselves to without asking for a receipt nor proof for our résumé nor insurance against damage, has lasted a lifetime. There are no formulas for accessing it nor unvarying programs.

Every chosen one must meet their furrier, with different knives. Mine was Walton's concerto for violin and orchestra and immediately afterwards, with astute and almost sadistic deliberation, Prokofiev's first. I cannot say that the Concorde flew direct and without delay to the glory of greater music, past the path of the innocent donkey in the children's song *Arroz con leche* or the dove in that sentimental and popular *vidalita*. No. May certain tangos forgive me my belated appreciation, which came thanks to the grace of certain voices, but I lived hours of silent fury while stuck in the birdlime of a catalog that an insufferable uncle of mine loved so much. Hours that

were required to slowly prepare the emptiness of a
great need which began to be filled during the fortu-
itous trance of listening to those concertos for violin.
They did not impose their law on me for no reason:
the moment had come for me to discover freedom
and submission all at once.

Long before that, every morning when we
arrived at school, we would wait for the bell to send
us to class and, after getting into formation – a sacred
word, an order that does not hurt anyone, that gives
our soul a human form, that allows children forced to
enter into the nongame of the adults to gather their
strength, to be with themselves for a few minutes –
we would file in to the rhythm of Mozart's *Turkish
March*, Beethoven's march from *The Ruins of Athens*,
or Schubert's *Rosamunde*. And through that marching
day after day, for years, we were imbued drop by drop
with a love for those works that I never grew tired
of, most likely chosen by the music teacher, a giant
dressed in black…

(No, it is not possible that the instant I wrote
this – I swear before any hypothetical and curious
reader – I started to hear that same march about
those same ruins. There is something I find discon-
certing. Of course, it is Beethoven's *Variations on
an Original Theme*, which he was well within his
rights to compose, suspecting perhaps that Liszt,
that loathsome man with crystalware included,
would come along ready to improve and use any
theme that was beautiful and not his own, like this
one from 'my' march. In any case, coincidences are
another matter, which I also consider to be 'mine'.
If there is any doubt, I offer this as a way to prove it:
Austin, Thursday, 5 March, 1998, two o'clock in the
afternoon, KMFA, the noble radio station that does

not subject us to advertising and is paid for by various types of benefactors, angels, patrons, large and small and deceased, whose memory we share because they loved music. I will now close this parenthesis that I could not help but open.)

Yes, a giant dressed always in black, but whose waist was brightened by the horizontal polychromatic stripes of a sash, Bulgarian like him. Recently arrived, having fled we all know what devastations, there he was, standing before us, and no one made a sound. He benevolently directed me past the doors and into the ignored world of music because I had been placed in the front row for humble reasons of my height and never being off key. While singing in the choir, something I would need for the rest of my life, I was happy, and it is possible that it showed. We sang, with ad hoc lyrics by national talents, what I later learned was *The Messiah* (pan... pan pa padapapanpapan, etc.), Schubert, Brahms. If Kiril Svetogorsky had come to us from Italy, we would have had Verdi – in those days nothing could have saved us from *Va, pensiero* – and I, who in the evenings was already often served my Italic and operatic soup in whose repetition to drown myself, could have hated what I instead loved.

This happened to me in some measure with the arrival of nationalism, represented by Vicente Ascone – who did not wear black and whose stature was more on the short side – promoting folkloric *vidalitas* and *pericones* and lyrics by Silva Valdés, all of it respectably naïve and scholastic. Was that the first injustice to which I was an unknowing witness? There I might have been destined for musical hell had I been more permeable. I think back with gratitude to that immense auditorium soaring upwards, three floors separating me from the skylight, and to Thalia and Saint Cecilia, who from their distinct sacred fields and with their magical team of secular collaborators toiled in harmony to salvage certain tastes. Nowadays I imagine the cultured educational body specializing in music must spin with threads considerably less fine than those and the end result is burlap or death, a *murga* of street musicians and with any luck some rhythm from Brazil, which it seems to me is better off when it comes to popular music. And other things...

But I was fortunate to have a Bulgarian spirit nearby, uprooted but bound to music's flawless reliquary. Although I believed I had found Walton and Prokofiev on my own, after whom I soon learned to conquer a field spangled with treasures, it is clear I owed it all to that teacher whose face I forgot from focusing on his hands that signaled our entries and his feet that involuntarily kept time and his voice filled with rolling r's, with a few precise words that were perhaps difficult for him. Also, his face was very high up because he stood on a small podium.

I have to admit that raptures of surrendering to beauty have never been more absolute than on musical occasions. Sometimes the allure of a portrait – shared by the model and the pictorial brilliance – gets its hooks into us and it hurts to pull them out (Antonello da Messina? Dürer?). Sometimes a landscape, that blue green of Patinir's waters or the golden chaos of one of Turner's skies, will forever move us. But that need for a deep breath, that expansion of our chest that feels empty, that ascent our soul pursues and from which we cannot break free, that 'unable to bear so much beauty', impossible to analyze, only with music. Only within music.

Yet this occurred with certain pieces I wanted to

listen to limitlessly, certain voices, a small collection, eclectic and rife with non-wisdom, that promised everlasting illumination. Radio Oficial's published program was my guide: on the day and time of the desired transmission I needed to be at home, hoping not to encounter any obstacles. Its neighbor on the dial, another broadcast, ecclesiastical, also offered musical wonders in addition to its morning masses. And if I connected the antenna, I received two other good transmissions from Buenos Aires. The discoveries that occurred modified my tastes and searches, accumulating portions of solid ground and new obsessions. I suffered for decades when my record of Schütz's three solitary *Sacred Concertos* was damaged beyond repair. At the time none of his other works had been recorded until the widespread discovery and worship of the baroque when he vaulted to his rightful place and those concertos became accessible and my memory could compare them with my recollection.

With the years came greater freedom and lots of music. The friend of a friend, slightly older than us, was a music critic. I had the luxury of one or various evenings of weekly music thanks to their relationship, which was more discreet in my presence. For years I attended every one of the many things the postwar era disaster sent to our shores. I felt compelled as if by some indisputable teacher not to miss any of that torrential course for which, to my eternal condemnation, there were no practicums.

I had heard albums by the Aguilar Spanish lute quartet. When they played together, they sounded like a rondalla. Tuberculosis, a disease that is still almost always fatal, a favorite of the war and its shortages, affected three of the four siblings. Paco, an extraordinary lutist, was constantly on tour so the others could rest in the dry, clean air of a sanatorium in Argentinian Cordoba. He even wrote *A orillas de la música* (On the Shores of Music), a delightful book about the quartet's relationship with contemporary artists, with Falla, with writers and poets. He came to Montevideo, possibly withered by the same disease. I discovered an instrument as well as Spanish medieval music, a prodigiousness that made me understand the frenzy some pop idols inspire in the younger generations.

The lute appeared and disappeared like a strange bird. In the meantime, my house revolved inside a different sphere. More precisely, it remained still and unchanged while I moved about a hideously empty space with nothing to grab onto. One afternoon after lunch, my aunt opened up the newspaper to have a look at it before heading back to the school. I read it only very rarely, but a headline stood out before my distracted eyes: it announced the death of Paco Aguilar, survivor of his three siblings. I could not help but read the article aloud. My aunt asked me very calmly and with a hint of sarcasm who the deceased was, and after my distraught explanation, muttered: 'He wasn't even part of the family.' I wanted to please her; I would have liked to break the iciness that respect sometimes places over affection. She never imagined her sentence would stay in my memory forever, although nothing appeared to have changed. The first thing I published 'consciously' were four sonnets, one of them dedicated to that deceased who was not 'part of the family'. There, too, my natural reservation regarding this was born, which I would start to write about, a substitute perhaps for the music that I was denied.

When I was a child, no one set me on the path to learning an instrument and then it was too late. But a concert in the Ateneo's modest music hall brought me face to face with another experience similar to Paco Aguilar's lute. The program began with old Italian arias followed by Schubert. I heard a voice that flowed like water. Never had a national soprano granted me such comfort. Olga Linne was the convergence of two schools of voice: the German and the Russian, exquisite timbre and perfect taste. I knew that I had to study with her, not because I could sing that way, but because that way of singing was a mystery I needed to be close to. At that moment and for three years, the cinema and my minimal splurges (the used books I picked out hardly cost anything) came to an end. I had just enrolled – pointlessly – in law school, and there was no one nearby with a piano to study. But I began my weekly classes with her. She sang *sotto voce*, correcting and encouraging me, even though there had to have been considerable distance between my meager efforts and those of her longtime disciples. One day I decided that parallel and distant paths cannot be traveled simultaneously and I quit, wisely and sadly. I was a devoted presence at her concerts, visiting her every now and then. The world was unaware of her, and it is possible that today very few people remember her. Her worst enemy was her great shyness, her extreme modesty. With the death of the Russian Goldenhorn, her teacher at St. Petersburg's Imperial School, she had no one to prepare with when she sang in public and had to travel to Buenos Aires. Despite her discretion and my inexperience, I managed to put together something from what she shared about her life. Her German

husband had abruptly vanished, leaving her with a
son and a daughter. One day in class she seemed
different to me, nervous, happy, distracted: the man
had reappeared, fifteen years after his departure, and
she was going to see him. I felt our roles reversed: her,
a naïve young girl willing to rekindle past suffering,
and me, skeptical beyond my years. But it was from
this purity and innocence that her voice emanated,
pouring forth with the same unwaning tenderness
well into old age, leaving me intolerant of so many
successful voices I find to be coarse, mere fruits of
technique. I will never be able to thank her enough
for that path of conscious enjoyment she illuminated
for me, the lesson of her selfless dedication to art.

Mutis, Álvaro

My dearest Álvaro: These days, marred by modernity,
we do not often write letters any more. Thank
goodness then that the telephone is at hand when
nostalgia intensifies. But thank goodness too that
someone who keeps track of sacred dates gives us
their voice, and has their say, on the commemoration
of your advent – not planetary, as one poet from my
country once called a simple birth, but Colombian
– thereby enabling so many of us to celebrate it
together. Of course, distance has done us a bad turn
devouring the time required to emulate Ariosto:
ladies, loves, knights, cats, because *arms* would be
excessive. And if the time available to us is a problem,
the place in which we make ourselves available is
no less so, because one would prefer the carnality
of affection that reaches out and embraces, a need
you will understand that surges and urges us from
these reformed lands and with cold, hard stars, where

spontaneity, an exclamation, a gesture, any sort of closeness are enough to be discredited.

Given the almost total absence of rights that for a time followed our image in the new mirrors of exile, all our sensitive pores thirsted for the water of empathetic affability. One day, which was a night, we stumbled upon an oasis or a waterfall. After a reading by Octavio, a group of friends went with him to a restaurant. In the end, someone with the resolve of a sheik whisked away the entire check. Marie-Jo Paz gave the perfect definition: *Mais ce Mutis c'est un volcan!* Igneous or not, from that moment on your image forever implied generous immoderation.

How can so much freshness accompany your infinite experience, so often recounted after a silence that undoubtedly revisits *the infinite vanity of everything* in some clever, and therefore skeptical, but always magnanimous conclusion? Lucidity usually consumes all the oxygen that the flame of generosity toward others requires. Not in your case.

Many times, it has weighed on my conscience that the energy we your friends have vampirized from you springs from the same source that feeds your work. But would the writing be the same if you had been born in prudent isolation?

There are those blessed few whose spirit gives life to a world that would not exist without them and whose greatest fascination comes from that ability. Since we have known you, I have found myself sticking my head in snares previously unknown to me: an imaginary Coello, a Jesuit refectory, quotations from León de Greiff, a card table where holidays and harvests are lost. These join earlier confirmed devotions we share like Larbaud, Proust, or Lernet-Holenia. There are of course inevitable bifurcations.

You carry Catalina Micaela in your soul. I have never settled the intriguing debate regarding Fabrice and Count Mosca. And since it has been so long since we were able to have our own pets, as they would hate our moves and urgent trips, and agreeing with Ibn 'Arabi that on judgment day even our clothing should testify for or against us and, even more so, our pets, I will perhaps summon the unforgettable Gaspar or wish to see Miruz's emblematic eyes one last time, to continue adding to my debts.

So many names unite in their admiration for Álvaro Mutis that I want to mention the first person I ever talked to about your work, in Montevideo, when *Elements of the Disaster* came out: the poet and dear friend, Clara Silva. Forcibly sedentary because of her age and especially because of Alberto Zum Felde's, when she found out we were leaving for Mexico, she was overwhelmed most of all by the idea that we might meet you. Had she been fortunate like us, she could have become one of the beings your life magnetizes. She was compassionate and sufficiently whimsical for that.

I am happy to think that the Almighty has not treated you unfairly. By bringing you to Mexico, he knew that here you were going to find everything: Carmen, and with the pleasant passing of time you would even welcome grandchildren, who since the days of Victor Hugo have complemented adventurous, fervent, Chateaubrianesque figures such as yours. And one more reason we owe you our thanks, that endearing Carmen, still able to look at the world around her while making sure you do not climb too high up the Tolima. A hug for you, a hug for you both. Austin, October 1996.

N

narcissus

And not at the water's edge; adorning the greenest, most vibrant meadow, they welcome Bach in his incandescent glory. From flower to Beguine, from Beguine to flower, the circle of silence then rises and surrounds us for several seconds of yellow, lavish, blossomed, hospitable eternity. In my memory there is a dream that resembles this wheel of serenity, this enclosure encircled by a reddish wall where the present is motionless and, even more moving, bygone times sit in impermeable immobility. The small houses, the small church, form a magical circle, at once limited and infinite. I remember, and nothing will convince me that remembering is not an exchange in which I leave something of myself there, forever wandering in some corner of Bruges during the season of the narcissus.

Nile

¡Qué triste era el Nilo!
Juan José Ylla Moreno

Timepiece of impartial ibises,
its ribbon-nervation.
Nile, silt that lost its motor,
knot now null, by inhumane science,
of death and life.

noise

Savage begins the noise that will topple
your castle begun in word masonry.
Long gone is the decrypted mystery
and the answer sought from the oracle.

At the doorway perhaps to the kitchen
of some angel we find very rarely,
you waited like one who waits anxiously
for injured miners in evacuation.

You waited, voiceless, for the drop or note
that would stem the stream of oblivion
to take you to that version now remote.

A car howls, a world that has lost its poise
screams your defeat day in and day out.
Enough. Shut up. Savage began the noise.

O

oblivion

Torrential, oblivion, that beneficent god, protects us, veiling from us the wounded zones of life. It descends in a protective rain over possible profiles of pain, over nostalgia, the awareness of decline or loss or any turbid form of evil, like in the winter landscapes of remote Chinese paintings, with mountains and chasms whose distances and depths are plunged into a fog that seems to conceal the dragon that emerges from the essence of the water. It sometimes also veils what could raise us to dangerous peaks of joy, Tarpeian rocks...

obsidian

Obsidius's Ethiopian stone, for me obstinately Mexican in its stubborn, dark interior, quick black fire. The blood of the sacrifices awaits, latent in its whetted lithic flakes, their festoon overseeing sanguinary celebrations, besieged brilliance falling drop by drop, obsessive, and darkening with indecipherable mourning, muted, a sacred secular field, a pyramid, other stones.

offertory

Chalice
with its slice of paradise served,
served chalice,
twice the paradise,
unappeasable peace.

Ophelia

Of all literature's non-malevolent characters, Ophelia
is among those who least move me, insipid, flowery
image of an innocence I find difficult to accept. After
all, the maniacal Hamlet is incessantly slipping her
hints of his constant obsessions and, misunderstood,
he mistreats her with his irony, which the prevailing
haze renders cryptic. Many sanguinary crimes
between literary couples are more dignified than
this march toward funereal madness, which Hamlet
insists on, without resistance from the victim. We can
accept that Polonius, the Obtuse, cannot see past his
nose, but a girl enamored to death should be more
perceptive, even assuming love's traditional blindness.

The Pre-Raphaelites often exalted certain
peripheries, macabre at times, and eternalizing
her on her journey toward aquatic death it suited
them down to the ground. Instead of 'the tiger in
the floating hyacinth' from *Tabaré* by Juan Zorrilla
de San Martín – that constant Uruguayan from an
early twentieth century they could not predict – they
saw Ophelia as an island of hyacinths, all of her in
flower, suspended in the more or less slimy waters of
a brook that Dante Gabriel Rossetti imagined lined
with bulrush and other bankside plants. The story
would have been different had Ophelia demonstrated a little weight and character, even a bad one,

and disputed the prince's assertions, neuroses, and compulsions, although in doing so she would have contravened the norms of the period. We all know this is what is most difficult, when the other expects the plodding aplomb of applause. Nevertheless, with other feminine characters, take Portia for example, the playwright proved to be more adept and less glowering.

The poor girl, incapable of asserting herself against Oedipus complexes and abusively demanding blusterers, did not prevent, through some timely, well-directed outrage, catastrophe's crowning with the tumbling of a crown. Restraint has its disproportions. Poor Ophelia, forever redheaded and floating, never having come of age!

opportunity

I remember, so many lustrums later, that bowl overflowing with pear compote, which did not wobble like this elastic sonorous succession. Composed, it cooled in the night dew on a windowsill, though behind precautionary bars, in some forgotten corner of *l'Île*. There were certain basic groundworks of young hunger, a stomach precisely aligned with the conventional timetable of daily meals and an unsettling misalignment with the brevity of these opportunities that left the desire for a gracious complement hanging in the air. In the meantime, one had to focus one's attention on the chestnut trees, the small, unexpected stairways, the usual cats, the lamppost beside the steps where sweet Nerval hung one night; mistakenly attend an improbable concert for castanets and harp (even if Laskine was playing the latter), very near perhaps to another hall where

163

the dual agony of Berthe Trépat and her spectator
might be happening; confront nasal and high-pitched
concierges; take note of the irritated couple, fed up
perhaps with the Cartier-Bresson imitators, who
mended wicker chairs against a wall so plastered
with old posters that one could imagine an Alphonse
Mucha hidden layers below. We ate early and little.
The night out continued for several more hours, and
a slight feeling of lassitude in our bodies reminded
us of their right to a modest portion of bread and
cheese each according to their needs. That particular
time the peacefulness of the evening in those narrow
streets, the Proustian world that was still discernible
behind those grand vestibules, in the cobblestone
patios, was adhesively perfumed with a memory of
well-stocked family kitchens, a powerful magnetic
pole that altered our course. But those pears were
someone else's. But they smelled so good. But meant
for other people. But they were seemingly abandoned.
But, alas, behind bars! That place tempting us so
appeared to be the kitchen in one of those select,
miniscule restaurants that on every corner offend
the calculations of needy scholarship students. While
Conscience and Hunger settled their dispute medie-
vally, our feet, trained to fulfill their humble function
without meddling in matters not incumbent upon
them, continued walking and resolved the dissention.
However, higher up we were persistent. And also
impartial: now that the temptation was behind us, we
left it to Moira to intervene. We would proceed with
our stroll, allowing destiny time to act in accordance
with justice. But if on our way back the bowl was
still there, tantalizing the world, then we would play
our roles. It is likely that we walked a little faster,
that we viewed the architectural offerings with new

distraction. There was a painter, a manual man, who, when the time came, furnished the tool for the crime, the unfolded penknife that carefully skewered the pears and distributed them honestly until all had been consumed. A hint of remorse accompanied the delicious fruits of our wrongdoing. We resumed our stroll, but a ghost interrupted our dialogue with the sights: the ghost of that fresh and distraught syrup whom we had robbed of its *raisons d'être* one by one, leaving it, unwillingly of course, to its pointless survival. And because we were not indifferent, besides the fact that we had not been able to enjoy it, it pained us to think that the careless chef might see such abandonment as taunting or disrespect, although I could not stop imagining how delicious the second batch would be when new pears were cooked in that same syrup for the customer who would order them.

origin

Maybe it all began in Sicily. Sicily was little more than a distance, an enormous one, that my paternal grandfather had crossed in a sailboat, advancing and retracing its wake in equal measure during a time that I placed in a past extremely remote from my own. And so the months transformed into a horrible ordeal, his only nourishment coming from the parallel multiplication of fish and bread, both dried: cod and hardtack. The former, forever loathed by the voyager and whose name alone caused him intestinal anxiety, disappeared from the family diet. In the field of national history, my grandmother was a declared Oribist (partisan of General Oribe, that is, the White Party) out of loyalty to her caste and, in doing so, stood in opposition to the paterfamilias's Colorado

Party tendencies, which were to be expected from a Garibaldian; but she upheld the cod veto, even decades after my grandfather's death. I imagine she accepted that she must never have liked it. Stigmatized by my forced ignorance of its flavors, I still get excited at the very mention of it which ushers forth mists of forbidden fruit.

But let us return to that faraway island. It took center stage by way of a surreptitious rosary that appeared among the laces, batistes, and madapollams of the undergarment drawer in my grandmother's large dresser and which she had partially hidden there many years earlier for superstitious safekeeping after rescuing it from the rubbish where my grandfather had tossed it. By looking at it, one could unstring the chronicle of her sister-in-law in its audiovisual version, in the sepia of an old image that held within its edges an almost treeless hill with a short, solitary house on top. It was there no doubt, among dismal and joyless farmsteads, where I placed the slim figure of Grazia, gorgeous, with her hair styled in graceful ringlets, looking at us with excitement for the future from another photograph. Her older sister, whose name was swept into oblivion because of the unpleasantness of her memory, sensed that allure's combustibility and willed the house to the church, like a dowry, to guarantee that after her death (perhaps foretold), Grazia would be admitted to the local convent for life. Her brother's resourceless anger was to no avail. Having left his native Nicosia, he had gradually lost, with each wave of that infinite journey, any right to dictate and intervene.

When my grandfather, still young, died unexpectedly, several of his many sons and daughters were adolescents or children. The seasoned eye of a gardener who had worked with the family in more comfortable times perceived in my grandmother what were for him the familiar signs of distressing necessity, concealed as is not usually the case with those who are born poor. He was about to return to his Sicilian lands and as a show of gratitude to his saints for the benevolences of 'America', he offered to communicate the bad news to that landowner, who at the time was still alive, despite everything.

When he returned, he sheepishly relayed the decisive and rancorous response. There was no assistance for her fancifully named sister-in-law, Galinda, or for the *nipoti*, whose names were even more fanciful. Over there they had heard that the progeny were not baptized. Along with a tolerable Miguel Ángel and a biblical but combative Débora, the names my grandfather had exhumed from Greek and Roman history (Publio Decio, Tito Manlio, Marc'Antonio, Rosolino, Pericles, Ida) and from Stendhal (Clelia and Fabricio) smelled of sulfur. Perhaps out of distraction, the one that was later passed on to me appeared in the calendar of saints, though this was mostly overshadowed by the importance of a mountain that favored the muses. In the end, it became clear that His Eminence had arranged everything with impeccable order.

The older sister fell gravely ill and, if a photograph of her existed, it must have been ripped in half by avenging hands. As the final moment drew closer, priests filed in and out of her bedroom, watching over her tirelessly without interstices or obstacles. They acted diligently, you must understand, at the possibility that the younger sister left behind might eventually deliver her hand and the hill and the house surrounded by vineyards into the hands of some wicked Carbonari. What else could you expect in those days, especially from a family that, while it contained good Christians, had also taken up the cross – oh, contradictory idiom – of a raging mason who in America, a vague out-of-control territory, had undoubtedly propagated that bad seed? Proficient in siegecraft, they likely convinced Grazia of the risks her beauty presented, of the devil lurking in her silhouette. Or they did not convince her. Maybe this devil, eager not to lose a soul he was said to hold powerful sway over, did in fact covet her, and precisely because they attempted to counter his ways, he won her when a destiny was forced upon her, one which I want to assume she did not desire.

Decades after those events, for me legendary, I had to study the Italian language, its beauty as remote for me as it was for my classmates of Spanish and English heritage. D'Annunzio, Ada Negri, Carducci, and so many others straightened up their spines from the bookshelves, but their calls fell on deaf ears because French had found me first. I was even somewhat annoyed when my declining grandmother would often ask about Italian words still unknown to me rather than consulting her own children. They had all gone to the Scuola Italiana. Almost all of them had forgotten what they had learned. In those days, for me Sicily was not yet Trinacria.

Later, little by little, I loved the Italian language. In it I discovered poets whom I revere, and I replaced, not without nostalgia, the direct knowledge of what I did not know of it with complementary versions, which I accumulated in sources that never cease to flow, in solfataras I hope will stay aflame for many years to come: Verga, Pirandello, Lampedusa, Piccolo, Sciascia, Bonaviri, Consolo, Camilleri…, in the images of refined and reserved sensuality that navigate in Antonello's dark backgrounds, the one from the Sicilian colony of Messina. And it continues to surprise me, like an unforgivable distraction by some Higher-Up, that Ariosto was Ferraresi, the same Ariosto who mingled his magic-mattered characters with almost-human others, moving them across a geography at the pace of the Hippogriff, from Ireland and France to the mists of the Mediterranean, concentrating them at the end on the premonitory island of Lampedusa, where belligerent justice is served and Orlando regains his wits. And I continue to feel a light tug at my soul every time I attach yet another merit to that unknown other homeland. The same too when I read the negative findings Sciascia unearths here and there through centuries and documents recorded in their ominous immediacy. In many of these I recognize what I already know so well: a daughter, granddaughter, great-grand-daughter society that did not originate in Spain. It is impossible to ignore the defects magnified by similar dual origins: the scrutiny of one's neighbor, envy, the desire to tear down. Something that may seem unimportant but which for me is not may have its origin there in Sicily: solo singing, ignoring the art and the pleasure of the choir (I say art to exclude that latest and celebrated extension of the Spanish *murga*, in which the freedom to be off-key and off-color is justified and accompanied by others).

Today I know it, now late, and I imagine inside its limits all the dignity of its abstentions and profusions: its spiritual richness, with no shortage of errors and traps, but offering beauty that pleads and endures, humble and supreme.

ostrich

The ostrich is a bird of intellect. Considering itself to be an essential winged creature, it suspects that envy and some vague sense of malevolence might pursue it, harass it, do it harm. Its head is its most valuable possession, loaded with discernment. Wisely, it hides it. And so profound is the ostrich's penetrative abilities that it can make it disappear into the ground as if it were a tree and its head the root. With its head safely in shelter – albeit partial, fresh, and humid – the ostrich thinks better, according to what it thinks thinking is. There it finds quiet refuge and everything nonessential disappears.

There, for example, the history of the ostrich's homeland and of other territories that influence it is not disseminated as it really is. Like other forms of knowledge, history weighs on the soul if it is to be accurately transmitted and interpreted. The ostrich, enormously light, almost entirely valuable plumage, detests the slightest increase in its gravity. Densities are of no use to it. It avoids, then, sources of information that are not the established ones and their critics, as well as registering contradictions, connecting the details it receives despite its rejecting of them, and, especially, anything coming from faraway if it has not been purified by some consecrated purifier.

On the rare occasions it emerges from its paltry hideout, it lets itself be charmed by *the air of the times*, that is, by the ideas that everyone is repeating, the donated thoughts that spare it the effort of producing them at home. In reality, they constitute a shared heritage, and nobody verifies its quality, nobody wants to devalue it since it belongs to everyone, even if it is being incessantly contaminated with history, a highly mutable illusion. Essential changes can occur in the world, changes that would force the ostrich to suspend its vain search for a space free of infection and activate its thinking ability, but it is prepared to be immune to incidents.

Its admirers await the twinkle of its retrenched thought, its polychromatic opinion on the basic modifications to its environment, the groundbreaking messages the world's instability would compel it to broadcast from its condition of excellence, for the instruction of the general public. But it is strange how the habit of inner stillness does not alter the dust cloud. It continues converging and can cease to be a whirlwind, fall in the wrong place, and form a mound that leaves the ostrich's head in eternal darkness.

This matter I revisit here for reasons unknown to me should not concern those latitudes where the land has not been given ostriches, only ñandus. Only.

P

pair

>Pheasant and owl,
>owl and pheasant,
>>together ablaze,
>alone lose their ways
>>beyond the sea.
>Nothing separates them,
>pheasant and owl,
>>owl and pheasant.

passage

Slowly and Maragall, the epitome of culturology and patience. A journey of a thousand miles begins with the first step. What to do with this unnarratable rumination? I left behind the impressionable eucalyptuses, never at rest, in Punta Gorda, started walking down bustling Bucareli, but I inadvertently turn towards Lavaca Street at the eccentric shop with mannequins in brittle poses and old silvery clothing, that will lift the veil of its mysteries not where I anticipate but in clarts unknown. Slightly closer in space-time, I understood that in crossing its meager threshold I had entered through fashion's back door, to salvaged and marketable rags: silks, velvets, ostrich feather boas, and miniscule rhombus-patterned vests from the forties. I retreat, past the black satin shoes with rhinestone buckles, across the old wood floors, seeking the sun of the street with the black grackles, intelligent and generally hated (not by me), toward a distant void where – *step right up, step right up, step right up* – I can almost hear Professor Sancy's proclamation, yelled at the top of his lungs on another luminous morning in a carefree Montevideo, just one more amid the irritated chatter and shouted enthusiasm that accompany the needy buying and selling, there where the Tristán Narvaja Street Market comes to life: necessity and not snobbery, chorizos and tiny colorful fish, Saint George's swords and pictorial monstrosities of impossible palingenesis, the firstfruits of nutritious vegetables, alongside keys to demolished houses and countless decoupled materials that lost their reason for being and sit in sorrowful wait for specific odd objects. 'Portions of dark species' over the ground dominated by dust circulate at the aphelion of normal life like the creatures they traffic in. In which of time's plazas will my passage end, what ruins will I ultimately embrace?

patience

I

Such inclination for nature, so much pasturing in it, so much nourishing its estimation must have been necessary for Hui-Tsung to study his partridges and paint them with delicacy, feather by feather, and for Fabre, also seated inside reality's cast, to record the very terrestrial customs of the dung beetle or the sinister epeira and carry out a contradictorily enormous task with discreet wisdom. Noble patience, almost all-powerful, the lone antidote to quotidian death, inner strife and, most of all, outer, the turbid whiplash of what subjects you to death in scalene progression, curved in constancy and not torpefied. Noble patience that would have saved Empedocles, 'exiled from the gods and wandering' for placing his trust in 'the delusion of strife'.

II

Patience is amorphous: it takes the shape of the disquiet that contains it.

perfectionism

Someone told me that once on a certain island there was a multitude of mosquitos, a plague of them in constant proliferation that drove the inhabitants crazy. An industrious government discovered that toads could provide the solution to their problem. We all know that the toad does not swap ponds just because, particularly if it means heading out to sea. They needed to be imported. Respected and well-fed, the toads multiplied. Each species of toad has its own song. Were the islanders surprised at the sudden sonorous variety, with perhaps orchestral effect? There are those odd individuals who enjoy silence. Having forgotten the mosquitos, they were annoyed by all the toads. Once again there were complaints. The mongoose is a nervous but trainable little animal, sworn enemy of the snake. And the inoffensive toad too. The island imported mongooses from India. For a time, they fulfilled their duty and dined on toad. But soon they discovered that the world also had chickens to offer them. Up until a while ago, the island that wished to improve their fauna had mosquitos, toads, mongooses, and problems with their henhouses.

periclitate

Perhaps 'periclitate' is not a word to be used lightly around the dining room table, at lunchtime, while unfolding your napkin across your lap between a quick little cough and a finicky glance at the main dish. For many reasons, it was impossible for me to consider this, the primary one being my age which limited me in that moment: eight, nine years old? And another, no less important: the uncontrollable fit of laughter that overcame me when I heard it. It coincided with drinking water, something that children often do to postpone that atrocious moment of 'starting to eat like an adult'. Long ago I lost a characteristic I was unaware I had and that I am unsure whether to regard as good or bad, but to which I owe more than a few uncomfortable situations. It is possible that this one I am sharing now was the first: I was 'tempted' and when laughter seized hold of me, it was not easy to stop, even though I was able to become two people at once: somebody who laughed and laughed and somebody who declared 'that's enough', without any outside support. But the first me was indomitable.

The conversation – whatever it was about – came to a halt, and everyone looked at me. There was an indisputable principle (as well as others): children do not speak at the table except to ask for something, please, with discretion. I was the 'children'. I do not recall if that principle was put on hold when my cousins came from out of town and, the majority now being visitors, the ratio of old to young was modified, becoming less unfavorable for the latter. In the shadows of a more consistent discussion, I believe we mounted a tolerated whispering, if we were discreet. But this time I was alone to assume the uncomfortable category of culprit, not for talking, but for committing the faux pas of spraying the table-cloth with my mouthful of water. To make matters worse, while they were looking at me, I continued to laugh uncontrollably. I could not explain what it was I found so funny, beyond comprehension: that a word never before heard was related to − I felt something even more intense: emanated from − my Uncle Pericles; that he had his own verb.

Over the years, I came to realize the tragic burden this individual, so important during my childhood, carried within. At that moment, with the perspicacity that time can dull, I felt we were the two closest people at that table. Even if it was because he too did not speak. Without sharing the restriction that applied to me, he too did not speak. Unlike me, he did not want to speak. As the youngest, my grand-mother's favorite son, he would play dumb if she asked him something or quickly took a bite of bread to justify his muteness.

If it was Aunt Débora who addressed him with some question he could not escape, since she was beside him, he gave a response that was concise and almost inaudible to everyone else. He conversed some with my father, who did not speak much either, but not at the table. And all because years ago he had stopped talking to one of his brothers, whom I was beginning to dislike. Did I instinctually sense that Pericles was also in a state of dependency? That despite being an adult, he was an adult not like the others, his kindness more obvious and vulnerable? I knew he had a heart condition, which would one day lead to his death, and that he had not worked for many years, though he was a great help to Aunt Débora around the house and took care of my grandmother.

I was of course familiar with the verb 'devour': the wolf tried to devour Little Red Riding Hood; in the other house the ants had devoured grand-mother's plants. The similarity between that verb and the name Débora, your typical aunt, could not have escaped me. But I did not find this the least bit funny, neither alone nor among people. I was convinced that, like the god only my grandmother spoke of, she too existed in a realm beyond ours and all things comical or absurd were alien to her.

In contrast, 'periclitate' – such a strange word – could only have derived from my uncle; it could even be the key to understanding him. It was hilarious, it sounded like how I imagined sleighbells would sound. A piece of music the radio used abusively in those days and that I loved, Ketèlbey's *In a Persian Market*, seemed to complement it perfectly. But how could I explain all this? What could I say? Did they expect me to be able to clarify all this confusion to myself and with words, what in rapid and secret succession had triggered so much inopportune giggling?

This insurmountable separation seemed to be the case for both parties. They waited for my return to normality and sent me to fetch a kitchen towel to tidy up my surroundings, without inquiring further into the motives behind the disaster. Did they suspect something? The family system fragmented uncom-fortable situations into small particles, easy to dilute without a trace. Or so they thought. In any event, I did not forget that episode or that word made indelible through its connection. I was not yet accustomed to seeking the assistance of the dictionary's twenty-eight volumes that would later rid me of some of my anxieties and plunge me deeper into others. It took me a long time to understand that a verb, despite its seemingly minimal cautiousness, is not responsible for the bizarre or culpable relationships that one can create for it.

perplexity

When he was very young, inexperienced and inauguratory, he imagined that nothing resembled anything else, and that life would offer him the infinite surprise and unlimited originality of human beings. As he got older, he became convinced that everything resembled everything else, that he was traversing an interminable parking garage, sequentially, without whims or frights, where each level repeated the fanciless design of the ones before. And so death came for him, precisely as a modern doctor had described it, in accordance with foresighted final ethics. In his dying moment, those who were by his side heard him let out a faint whistle. Was it amazement, at last, having reached his supreme embassy on the other side, at something unexpected he was glimpsing there? Perhaps that whistle was an abridgement of Charles-Louis Philippe's last words when, in identical circumstances, he peered through his monocle at what no one else was able to see: *Nom de Dieu, que c'est beau!*[23] Or was it frustration upon

---

23 My God, how beautiful!

confirming, once more, that everything was just as he had supposed in so many stark moments: equally vain and specular? He never knew that this hardly solemn scholium of his was for those witnesses the elevation he had been seeking for himself: the irreproachable clamor that sets thought forever in motion around the heart of an unsolvable question, which for that very reason becomes essential.

poetry

I

Words are nomads; bad poetry renders them sedentary.

II

Reducing poetry to its maximum expression is unforgiveable. 'Less is more,' understood Mies van der Rohe.

progress

Seeing as how we live in a civilization of progress, it is typically considered reactionary not to accept the idea of progress. It forces us to state that the twentieth century is superior to the nineteenth century and that one to the eighteenth century and that one to the seventeenth. We must continue retreating in time in blind fulfillment of that assumption, which for many is law. The slow labor of our ancestors can thus be pitied since their achievements appear tremendously futile from atop the summit where such ascensional mechanics place us. We set off from those advances but, like the mountain climber who sent each of his footholds rolling downward, either from carelessness or because they were too unstable, and finds himself with no support below him, we now have a void behind us. Not everything accomplished by our century is compatible with what our predecessors thought. It matters little to us. The latest ideas are the good ones, the previous ones must be wrong, though they have served to hold up our – for a very short time – privileged thinking. The idea of a moral advancement is rarely defended. However, on higher scientific levels, the general idea of progress has been superimposed by science's specific idea of it, which appeared destined to be carried out at the expense of the sense of mystery, recovering principles that some had abandoned, as surprising as the breakthroughs in physics or biology may be. The frontier they seem to approach is always retreating. Could this mysterious retreat be what saves us from the thoughtless frivolity of the most vulgar idea of progress?

prowl

Prowl is a sordid word. It contains animal scents and movements. A thief prowls around a house. A jackal prowls and sniffs after the gazelle, its potential victim. I do not apply it to the aimless wanderer, to the footsteps following a path that does not exist until it is walked, so often with propensities for magic.

The most natural profession in the world seems to me to be that of the gold prospector, whom I always think of as an *orpailleur*, since panner is less precise and not always understood. All of us are searching, all the time, in order to find. And what we reach, distinct for every search, is the ultimate gold.

I can imagine Mozart in a carriage, no doubt, always rushing toward the next piano; but the German Romantics would likely prefer to walk after what they are searching for and that is how I picture them. The image that first comes to me, when something makes me remember them, is a dark silhouette with an overcoat and long hair ascending a precipice against a sea of fog, leaning on a walking stick, in a backlit painting by Caspar David Friedrich. It could be Goethe wandering Italy in search of the primordial plant or tree; or Chamisso or Jean-Paul, in search of themselves; the Brothers Grimm, from village to village, after the folk tales they are compiling; or William Hazlitt, through English hills and valleys, primarily after his desired solitude.

And none of that sounds like prowling. They were going. We can roam the unfamiliar streets of a city in search of something, oftentimes without knowing what. We fulfill our duty to search, trusting that the chosen route will fulfill its duty to offer. Our gaze advances summarily, not yet opening its doors to memory. Something suddenly receives it. Sometimes it is horror: a person with a monstrous bottom lip and, frightened, we forget that being imperturbable is not always indifference; it can be kindness. Other times, there is a shared smile and an impalpable embrace; we stopped at the sight of grace and are delighted to have noticed it: a young child or a friendly dog. Or it is an absurdity, now registered forever: in Padua, a home garden glistening with steel. Steel pergolas, steel railings, steel for the trellises... One would expect paths covered in tiny pebbles cast in that same material. Perhaps there are none because they are portable and metaphorical... I do not want to think about the effort the plants must make to wrap themselves around these inhospitable structures that will sear them in the summer and make their winter even more freezing. It is impossible not to begin imagining the mental source of this meticulous eyesore: A manufacturer utilizing their product, perhaps the surplus? A new Shylock who has collected a debt in kind and is using it to murder his garden, making it a prison and torture for the space and anyone who looks at it? Whatever the case, there the image has remained for chilling nightmares.

Sometimes 'the past' does not 'close like coffins'[24] and preserves a nonextinct species, which I do not mistake for the traveler, be it Chatwin or Manganelli or Vila-Matas. It is that wayfarer who embarks on pure discovery, with no safeguards. The protagonist of a charming and very modern novel, *The Year of the Hare* by Arto Paasilinna, walks across Finland without a plan, in the hands of destiny, more in nature than in cities and accompanied by an injured hare whose healing has tamed it, which will become both the journey's cause and one of its misadventures since it is against the law there to possess wild animals. W. G. Sebald achieved fame after his death thanks to his scrupulous record of autobiographic fragments, often linked by the never superfluous stitch of coincidences, a stitch usually sewn on foot. And he walks so much through the streets and parks that one day, seeing himself eyed by the doorman of the hotel where he is staying, he realizes, dust-covered and his shoes in tatters, that he has become indistinguishable from a vagrant. Jacques Reda collects on his constant walks the subtly varied material for his successive books in which he wends his way across countrysides, roads, French villages, on foot or bicycle, encountering

---

[24] Delmira Agustini.

uphills and cloudbursts, or the streets of Paris, where he refines his observant analysis until extracting astonishing images that materialize just that once for his incisive gaze. I read him without expecting uproar, little more than the ultrasound of his extreme attention that affords me the pleasure of unhurried variations.

More than twenty years of letting my eyes amble through the great oaks I see from my window have sharpened my receptivity to the minute litany that varies only in tone, patience and impassivity, with no other alarm than a bird rising from the branches or the changing colors of the leaves according to the seasons. But something from that visual prowling always remains. The word in which the writer rescues ideas and emotions remains. An unforgettable sketch by Dürer, rarely a landscapist, remains. The prodigious Chinese drawings that the Japanese will later expand into distinct styles remain. The backgrounds of Flemish paintings, of Tuscany, remain. What will the art of these past decades leave in matters of landscape, of a century that has destroyed and rejected so much?

R

reading

I

A burning mirror where what we consume consumes us.

II

The order of the factors, that one which does not alter the product in arithmetic dogma, is indeed capable of changes when applied to readings. Some of these should occur at a particular stage of life. It is desirable that fairy tales accompany us in our early childhood, and the norm is that they later take their leave. Sometimes they reappear with the vigor that winter seasons prepare; for me, slyly at first, sheltered by the prestigious name of Lord Dunsany or in collections: stories and legends from India, Ireland, Russia. It cannot be a sin of adult intellect when Italo Calvino put so much love into compiling ancient Italian fables, as did Alison Lurie into editing English fairy tales, modern ones in this case.

There are works capable of bringing together generations with distinct interests. I celebrated my eleventh year embracing a monumental package with novels by Jules Verne, chosen by me, one title after another, with looks of growing concern and uneasiness on that face urging me to proceed. All those books in paperback and in two columns undoubtedly cost the same as one or two in hardback and illustrated, but the idea of the book-object did not cross my mind, not even the possibility that shape, size, color, or the quality of the paper and the printing were elements worthy of attention. I thought only of the quantity, and so I considered that to be the most memorable gift of my life, an excess I was sure I would hear about. My very self-interested obedience to that encouragement by Eulalia, my aunt's friend turned circumstantial patron, would not be seen as conformity but rather abuse. And that is what happened, but I believe it was merely to satisfy the ritual of my ceaseless education. Soon my grand-mother became interested in everything Verne. With much restraint, she asked to borrow one book after another, and she was not the only family member to share in my gift, something that gave me a certain amount of pride.

I am not sure what age is appropriate for the painful reading of De Amicis. The family copy's state (of care), with engravings and escaping pages, revealed its years of use. Forgetting the generosity with which I lent my belongings, there was always an adult eye monitoring my handling of those loose pages, ensuring they were returned in the proper order.

The grief-stricken climate of all the stories in *Heart* assumes recipients who are already acquainted with the sorrows that lurk inside life's every step, preferably during our younger years, according to him. Or virgins of such sorrows but whose genes are prepared for them. Given the austere pedagogical style in those times, literary virtues were subordinate to a lineage's longstanding ethical education, principally Italian and still faithful to nineteenth-century values.

Much, much later, when De Amicis's importance to me lay mostly in my memory of the circumstances surrounding his reading and in the saturation of nostalgia that emanated from it (able to beautify years which were not so insolent as to be altogether beautiful), I witnessed a colleague in Mexico to whom I had ascribed the most sophisticated of devotions violently declare his loyalty to the Italian writer. On De Amicis's anniversary, or the anniversary of that book, a well-known television journalist who often allowed trickles of culture into his very popular daily program added a pompous note to his allusive words, an obvious concession to the tastes of a highbrow sector of his listeners. He had no sooner finished dismembering the Italian than he received a phone message from Salvador Elizondo. Visibly pleased, he aired the words of that unexpected and valued collaborator without warning. We instantly heard the most violent of interjections Mexicans use to allude to a dubious birth: Elizondo defended *Cuore*'s maligned merits. I do not know if his reading of it had been revised or if, like mine, it dated back to his juvenile and sacralizing years. Just the same, I loved his outburst even if it was not as pure as Garrón's very heroic ones, that model paladin positioned almost beyond what is the human.

recollection

Recollections are life, it is true. But what do we do when, beautiful and unpredictable, they march to an unfamiliar score and resist enduring relationships with the real pillars of our existence, with the passage of that primordial monster we call time in its spatial tomb, when they do not appear to have the fatality of the past behind them? What name should we give to those surprising sources of evocations that invent rather than reflect? Continuity with no beginning, indication of a stealthy nucleus arising perhaps not from life but from nocturnal parentheses, from dreams. The Greeks complied with dreams in which they believed they had discovered a divine origin, but they also revered deceitful dreams: it was difficult to know from where any of them came. The latter category, the only one still with us today, can cause cruel nostalgias to descend. Their nucleus seems to be some earlier event whose beauty is fit for turning an insipid future glorious, however long this may last. A moment later the bubble vanishes. The dream is accepted in that ephemeral state. But what of the memory that nourished it? We want to run to its rescue, verify its beating heart, accord it a radiating force that, from the oblivion to which we had relegated it, is capable of creating the illusion that served as its cocoon and vehicle until it faded. We are reluctant to admit that it is made of the same deceptive matter as the rest, that despite our experience of its apparent flesh and blood, it will disintegrate in an instant. Because, as we all know, nothing is more difficult to retain than a dream, wherever it may come from, save for that phantom evocation, equipped with inexplicable generative power.

Redon, Odilon

Deorbited eyes,
closed eyes,
cyclopses, chlamydes,
shadows or mysterious arcades
and radiant pegasusses in the heavens
and clouds?
     Water rises
from rotting kingdoms,
cold slime covers the dreams
of that man who dared.
Patient Parca
suckling death
sends tenebrous messages
from purple blues,
corollas and corollas.

return

A city does not forgive those who move away for a long period of time, especially if they were born in it. When they return, it will offer them strange erosions. During their stay it floods with rough and invisible waters in which the deserters are hopelessly shipwrecked. While the others advance untroubled, they must be wary of whirlpools and fissures. The peacefulness of other people's promenades is for them a potential seaquake. Corners that were curves grow sharper, advancing useless points of view emitted by aristarchs and zoiluses. The calmest of sidewalks becomes a zodiac. If one day a true swell occurs, a life-saving sandbar will await the constants, there where they will not be able to set foot. Perhaps in the name of their inner freedom, they will reject the knots of possible salvation. They then run the risk of being submerged to lethal depths. However, all absentees have the right to adventure, compelled by an absurd feeling of hope. Everyone has the right to return.

revelation

In the camera obscura of revelations, light opens a red slit and the soul is roused. An impious lamp has opened the path to a Styx that floods what was once a peaceful night. We went blindly but without risk of danger through the faithful known, sculpting the divined – silhouetted – shapes of life. Now what?

road

I

Every direction flies in the air and dies on land. A road is a caged bird, ground-stricken.

II

Many roads advance,
perfervid yet accidental.
But when traveled
traversed with victims, we suffer
among the wavering of devious pavements,
trifurcations forcing choices,
revelations of treacheries.
When the voice that advises
our errors has been deprived.
Then, like a viaticum,
we arrive at ourselves,
that place in the voracious wind,
where you must not linger.

S

Sabine

The celebrated Sabine women / are crying, they cry / because while fleet of feet / not all arrive at the moment of the abduction.

(*La sagesse Delacroix*)

sadness

Tristesse d'Olympio, Tristitiae rerum, Tristes tropiques, Tres tristes tigres, Tristeza não tem fin. Why does this word first bring me these associations, coming from far away, with precipitation of little consequence, that have lost sight of the anguish in which their definitively welded unions were forged? Our own associations are overlaid after the game, under cultural lamina, on the other side of the die we try not to look at but that sends us its sharpened points, nails for a secret crucifixion. And yet sadness is that slow woodworm, that faithful dog, capable of decennial patience, gnawing gently at our insides, waiting for injustice so it can dismantle the final layer and explode in a point overflowing with dolorous density.

Point? Tract? Is there in fact an exact boundary where sadness begins? Before it, perhaps, is melancholy, tolerable, almost desirable: it combats emptiness, sensibility is shaken and can be recorded in works. After it, never-ambivalent pain, blowing to pieces intentions, spirits, the mysterious energy needed for everything that is not 'tossing the blanket to the floor / and filling yourself with sleep'.

saxifrage

The lesson of the saxifrage:

                              blossom

through rocks,

                    be bold.

Scorpio

The eighth sign, second in the water trinity.
Scorpion, phoenix, or serpent?
The eagle excluded.

seedbed

We realize the utility of seedbeds when, after casting a resentful glance across a garden intent on the green spectrum, we hastily and paying little attention to the almanac buy various packets of non-lysergic seeds with an imaginary future: red or orange marigolds, blue or lilac larkspurs, purple flax, white lobelias, and sow them orderly in soft, propitious soil. This plot does not necessarily have to belong to us, but we should have lawful access to it for watering purposes. It is not essential we do this ourselves, but of course a devout thumb, if green, assists its plants. Now and again some climatic contretemps breaks that lets us observe the germs' reactions and our own. My experience indicates anxieties when the moment, sometimes lethal, of the transplant arrives; as well as the ominous excrescences of persecution from a trenching cat, and then a period of abandonment, difficult to avoid, during which the need to attend to other matters that may include previous seedbeds and their possible resurrections flows forth and leavens with astounding speed.

Later, it would be better not to speak of the soundless release, the mournful acedia with which the small monotonously green shrubs bring our wait to an end by sprouting barely visible watery scales, specks of faint coloration incapable of altering the course of any insect or compensating all our work with the hymn of their minimal hint of perfume. Soon after, they lose their petals, while the never-pampered geranium's proletarian splendor shines more precipitous, indelible, and friendly each day.

seism

Indomitable merciless minotaur rattles the unfathomable cavern where no Perseus manages to defeat it. Like the size of the moon in the sky, like the distances on a map, like the speed with which blood completes its tour round our fear, it is unclear how long the silent outburst lasts. By the time the subterranean effusion calms, we will have already abandoned the possibility of simultaneous thought, all of us intertwined with the disquiet that loses, in an unreal calculation of the future, the uninspiring tale, more pallid each day, of this confinement, for once nocturnal, to which we concede.

serpent

The serpent sparkles, free of dust;
it chooses a fruit,
not necessarily an apple:
a plum, a small nispero.
It suffices for it to smile, generous,
offering us every garden:

the four rivers stand still
and a bell will begin to snow
upon the world.

siren

In memory of José Durand
and his *Sunset of Sirens*.

Amid Gómara, Anglería, and Oviedo,
Durand moves from sirens to manatees
with lyrical-scientific pomp and show
and mythologizing zoologies.

Since all things reach the end, the afterglow
is filled with these sirens, raging fits and pleas
for the last few to unite in the know
and save sirenians in the cold seas.

Science I accept, like at Eucharist,
from those who rescue what they adhibit.
Still and all, the pirouetting manatist

does not my faith in the dolphin inhibit:
this precious sunset declares solemnest
the great merits their species exhibit.

skepticism

I

God of controversy,
let me forget
the lies I once believed,
grant me forgiveness
for the truths I maintain,
those which a turn of the earth
may make false.

II

Can something be known forever?
Nothing is embraced as forever,
soul inflamed since forever.
If scenic clearings, you'll have clearly seen...

space

Ball and chain is this space
that binds us,
cruel spouse, inverse wellspring.
No wings exist to cross it,
just one freedom:
our judgment that slowly
grows feathers from the errors of others,
from the invisible rein
that restrains us,
as if air alone were not enough.

sparrow

Three absurd sparrows
sing inside the fog
that smells of lemons.
The evening is empty

of gloomy, human hustle.
Alone, avian glory
gives meaning,
despite everything, to the world.

stones

Within the natural kingdoms, the levels of beauty in inanimate objects are not the least admirable. A stone's beauty is no less than that of a tree. Max Ernst wrote in a letter: 'We [he and Giacometti] are working with large and small granite rocks from the moraines of the Forno Glacier. Polished by time, ice, and weather, they look fantastically beautiful just as they are. No human hand can do this. Why not therefore simply leave the initial hard work to the elements and content ourselves with scribbling over them the runes of our own mystery?'

I have always been drawn to what an absurdity in our expression calls unfinished stones and suspect that I have given them more, and more astonished, attention than any jewelry store window. At the National Museum in Prague, I remember enormous opals larger than my open arms could embrace and seemingly on fire, the crow blue color of pyrite's geometric constructions, the veined labyrinth of immense slices of agate, and how I traced unhurried trails through countless and solitary galleries, guided by my astonishment at so much light and so many nameless colors. Any attempt at their definitions would only diminish them with approximative explanations. The resources for lapidary perfection are many, not just smoothness and luster, not just their floral hues. The rose rock has a muted ashen color and a surface of fine grains of sand that allow it to go unnoticed in a desert or on a beach. Its virtue stems from its calcareous petals, whose facets intersect, appear, and overlap; from the silent din of that clash of rhythms, senses, and directions happening on a small battlefield, those contradictory impulses produced by a strange conflagration at its center. Some predestined lands conceal geodes of delicate inner beauty. It takes an astute eye and certain clues to know that their unexciting exterior, round and pitted with whitish dimples, exposes a hollow center when split, a heart of air preserved among tiny crystals light blue, pink, and gray in color. Even before Surrealism, in the voice of one of its creators, recognized the potential for mystery in mountain rocks, there were already intense relationships of forces, powers, and sublimity between man and stones being formed. In the pre-Celtic henges or in the monoliths that manifest divine power for diverse primitive peoples, beauty is never absent. It is well known that in Japan some magnificent gardens replace their trees and grass with stones and sand. A rake traces vast parallel circles or complements them with tangential ripples, creating a geometrical well-being, which transforms space into an element to observe, not to traverse; the lines are not arbitrary, they are an artistic design that follows the contours of large stones, venerating their unadorned shapes. The center of this beauty is a rock, aridity offered as an absolute point of departure for thought. Many times, we have seen someone on a peaceful shoreline absorbed in their contemplation of a pebble or collecting, and cherishing, an ordinary stone smoothed by water and time. This is not a Buddhist garden, and yet they too have achieved a moment of serenity thanks to the humble beauty of a shape, of a color they alone value and rescue. A page should also be like a beach that offers opportunities to pause. I will place here, like a greenish sea-worn cobble or like one of those mysterious flat gray stones with a white line obeying the golden ratio that we find on some Italian beaches, the name of Roger Caillois, because of his collection of minerals (now in Paris's *Jardin des Plantes*), many of them, especially the astonishingly patterned quartzes and agates, extracted from the basaltic subsoil of Uruguay.

storm

The sweltering summer devours its own roses, lavishes us with jasmines and oxidizes them. A cat lost in thought emanates an intolerable, incoherent smell of old fish across the lawn. The Chilean salt has tinted the grass a Rousseauian (adjective with three fathers) aniline green and now it contrasts with the pale slate-blue sky in which a false horizon of mountains has suddenly ascended, with portly, reddish clouds settling in with congressional slowness to watch the arrival of the storm. In the south, a malevolent relationship exists between the northern wind and these tensions that, while all the sky's latent darkness readies its ambush, lift any ordinary object into the air, a scrap of paper, which gains an identity and a moment of splendor. They let fall, however, the electric deluge that piles the most ephemeral of summer's beauties against the walls: mounds of unexpected hailstones. And we seek shelter behind a window and consider the traps laid for our trust, by cats, almanacs, skies, and occasionally, because of the gravity of experience, by human beings.

superstition

'Feeling of religious veneration, based on fear or ignorance, that often compels a person to develop false obligations, to be afraid of illusions, and to place trust in things lacking in power. Futile omen derived from chance accidents. *Fig.* Excess of precision or caution in any matter.' I take this partial definition from the *Littré*. Bloch and Wartburg state: 'to remain beneath'. To subjugate? Briefer still, Corominas gives little more than its etymology: 'survival'. I admit to being superstitious, a fanatic of precision, never achieved, and I detect opposing viewpoints in these two etymologies. B. and W. look at the superstitious individual and see someone who is sheltered, subjugated, or perhaps overwhelmed by superstition. Corominas reflects on this belief and is perhaps amazed that it survives.

Have I confessed to being superstitious? Perhaps turning these relationships over in my mind will help me see those I might have with one, or various, superstitions. Have I subjugated myself to them? Do they survive in me? The first one I remember is late and hardly original: I can picture myself on the way to school, determined to walk along the granite curb that bordered the sidewalk, one foot carefully in front of the other because straying from that straight line meant disaster. I suppose this disaster referred to some lesson I was yet to learn and the ocular marksmanship of the teacher who would notice it, such that it must have seemed to me, indeed, irrational and magical. Sometimes the minefield was not the dangerous curb; I had to avoid the risk of stepping on the cracks between one paving stone and another, all while walking at a normal pace; taking care not to save myself with some dishonest forward thrust, just barely clearing it, or the contrary, that some deceleration did not detain my foot already destined to place me in danger: the crack should fall in the middle of my stride. I read *Confession de minuit* years later and internalized poor Salavin's obsessions. At almost the midpoint of this little novel, Georges Duhamel offers the pages dedicated to a meticulous description of the compulsion with which his protagonist exacerbates his problems while he searches for a job that might free him from a dead-end situation. He too counted paving stones or imagined a precipice at the edge of the sidewalk. It did not trouble me to see my little superstition exalted in literature as a symptom of manic depression. In the end, I have never been a depressive and by the time I discovered Duhamel, I no longer gambled on the rise and fall of sidewalks.

Numerical superstitions are among the oldest in the world. Since I generally forget what day it is, I have not been able to incubate concern for the 13th, something so commonplace that the great Hotel Moksva, across from the Red Square in the heart of the orthodox USSR, was without a 13th floor (in its numbering, of course, because no way could they remove the material passage from the 12th to the 14th). But in a time of frequent widespread catastrophes, attributable to the chaotic political situation in my country and not to humble individual relationships with bad circumstances, I must have on more than one occasion ascribed each day's problem to the conjunction of a Tuesday and the 13th, traditionally worrisome and always up to date. But how can we prove the true power of a number when there were other forces at work under which many of us endured, to our dismay? The apprehension felt throughout a long flight on Tuesday the 13th (a date when it is easier to find tickets even in periods of normal traffic) and during hurricane season is nevertheless justifiable: this is always a reliable source of anxiety. I was not infected with other superstitions. José Bergamín had a curious one, perhaps commonly Andalusian: on hearing the word 'culebra' (cobra), he immediately stood up, grabbed a chair, and began to spin it on one of its legs; to the left or to the right, I do not recall which, and this was perhaps important. Every once in a while, someone let that little word slip and he would rush towards a chair, his slight irritation assuring us that it was no joke. But I do not know of anyone who adopted this compulsion, more onerous than 'knocking on wood'. What do we do when there is no protective chair close at hand?

If it is a matter of choice, then I am in favor of any superstitious belief or practice. All of them. In moments when the past is disappearing with greater speed; when ties are being cut with traditions, etymologies, duties; when books, dreams, courtesies, and noble acts of kindness are being forgotten; when pessimism is the order of the day (and I would not say unjustifiably so), superstition acknowledges that evil exists and proposes modest defenses. If anyone wants to restore its formula, I will offer them this one, austere and cryptic, handed down from a calamitous Saturn, planet of plagues. I take it from *Piers Plowman*, a book written by William Langland at the end of the fourteenth century: 'When you see the sun displaced and two monks' heads in the heavens, when a Virgin possesses magic powers, then multiply by eight and Plague shall withdraw and Hunger will judge the world…' Confronting the warning signs of new catastrophes, so clearly foreseeable, with no other task but to multiply by eight is not bad, although we first need to identify the multiplicand. And stock up.

syllable

Pirarajú, piragua, Piranesi,
swaggering passing paladins,
passerine prisms imprisoned
in seditious sibylline syllables
that gather their enigmas.
Heraldic dragons on a shield that fortifies
arcana for the blind.

symmetry

Death forgets its own existence with offensive serenity, knowing that any symmetry involves it.

T

telephone

It sometimes bursts into the silence with a short noise and then regrets it; we have already turned our backs on it when it raises its resounding outburst, a bountiful proclamation announcing who knows what wonders. It can suddenly emit false voices, generate false lightning strikes, make the room tremble like an earthquake, cry out, offer, rave, lament, retreat, return with the wind. It represents the unstable pulse of possibility, it toys with you and with the secret indigence with which you watch for jolts, surprises. We must run to it if we are far, placating it with a look that acknowledges its demands until we arrive. If it is black, tensely pristine like a funeral car, we cannot help but fear news that will fall upon us like a merciless mob to brutalize the left side our chest. But if it is one of those white models that have descended from the kitschy films with enormous interior staircases to the disguised vulgarity of the office place, or if it has novelty colors like red, green, cream, or it replicates stone patterns, or its inner workings light up, then we might expect of it something like a flower or an acoustic arabesque, a joyous gilded fly that signals pleasant things, kind invitations, offerings of good fortune, or the caress of a fond memory, itself sufficient enough. In times of exasperation, skepticism, we make it an accomplice in the world's gloom and maliciously leave it to exhaust its unattended roar, to shroud itself with a silence that does not startle. Then it weighs on us, reflecting our quiet cowardice. Now without discretion, on any day, including the once-sacred Sunday, it proffers imperious or cloying voices at any hour that threaten or propose something, veiling the insult of assuming our submissive stupidity. For a while, we were consoled by our disdain or urging them not to insist. They soon arrived sheltered inside a recording. We hang up, knowing a new inevitable call will come, at any hour.

theater

At a certain age we realize that multiple theater scenes are taking place around us. The most precocious notice this as children; they discover secret rigging systems and then commit what adults consider terrible indiscretions. In return for their perspicacity, they receive anger and punishment. The slower ones are adolescents when they reach this same state. They can become definitive skeptics. Some decide to accept the revelation and exorcize it. By seeing traces of theatricality in everything around them, they hone a special sense of vigilance. They isolate false gestures, artificial tones, tirades declaimed after opportune rehearsals. They register and record all this, giving it perhaps excessive importance. They eventually formalize their pursuits: one day they join others affected by the same obsession and compose a theater troupe with which they intend to offer the fruit of so much observation in exchange for the pleasure of seeing the world from the stage, themselves in lights.

Rewarded with a school that accepted the incessant challenge of the latest pedagogical developments, I participated in three early and minimally compromising scenic experiences, in what could be considered a theater for the masses in miniature. In the first of these I was a ghost of darkness cast out by Prometheus's fire. I needed to cross the stage dressed in lilac muslins and a tall conical hat, indisputable ghostly attributes. Ercilia, the school's dutiful caretaker whom my aunt had charged with accompanying me to buy the fabric, let me add a few dazzling rhinestones that had little to do with the shadows from which I would be wrenched. I was not alone; I was part of a row of dispirited ghosts, all of us with our hands supposedly tied behind our backs. Some of us had to speak a line that ranged from mono- to pentasyllabic. Emboldened because mine exceeded the simple 'ooh', when the spotlight momentarily reached my place in that taciturn chain, I said it and in a sudden stroke of inspiration, raised my arms over my head for greater expressivity. I was no doubt enveloped by a rush of pride at the thought that it had not occurred to our drama teacher to include a gesture so greatly elevating the importance of my phrase. From the darkness, I heard the sound of laughter. The audience had perceived that by effortlessly breaking my invisible tethers, I had also broken a plot line to which my companions in captivity remained obedient.

In the second experience, I was a caravel. It was October 12, of course. They had directed me to rock back and forth, in such a way that made me appear ill-fated to simulate my advance across the raging sea, over the hard and slightly dusty floorboards of the small stage in the school's assembly hall, to the rhythm of a song I remember to this day, still anonymous. I was not expecting to be Columbus, but I confess I was mortified not even to be among the indigenous, to be an object, albeit a beautiful one and part of a decisive triad. I did not give my all to this role. And also, when the curtains opened, I already had a splinter in one knee.

My third experience had more emotive aspects. I was, for the first time, part of the Exodus of the Uruguayan People in an epic work from the never-idle pen of our perennial author, Humberto Zarrilli, who this time had abandoned Aeschylus as his source of inspiration, seizing instead on H. D. (Hermano Damasceno, from whose pleasant version of our national history, in a copy handed down to me and on my own, I gained knowledge that would later be demolished by tendentious individuals and recon-structed into new configurations, undoubtedly also incorrect but less picturesque). Uruguay is a small country in American dimensions, though not so small that wagons were not essential to the Exodus. But they would have increased staging costs beyond what was reasonable. Therefore, they rolled along somewhere else or had gone by just before the curtain was raised. We constituted a pedestrian mass; in reality, we were the emotional parade of those who with more love and true sacrifice followed Artigas, the Father of the Nation, on his journey north, leaving the empty land fertilized with the blood of our lacerated feet. I made one pass with a bundle resting on my head, twirling the ruffles on my red percale gaucho dress as much as I could. I ran behind the stage so I could reappear dragging something but with nothing on my head, merging with the unattainable ambition of that seemingly vast multitude. I once again ran backstage to rejoin them, this time in the front row, standing out from that mass turned amorphous thanks to my fleeting prominence. Now I was carrying in my left hand, the one facing the audience, a prop of my own invention, finally acknowledged and accepted by the stage director: a birdcage with my Roller canary, who did his part in solidarity and sang as if inspired by the sacred boards.

Both of us abandoned them for good after that. Since then, I take the seat of the spectator, with less and less enthusiasm, while continuing to be attentive to that other, everyday theater, without applause or lights or much imagination, in which we all participate whether we want to or not, monotonous from the inane and constant repetition.

time

Contradictory wheel of always harnessed changes, of stillness that spins about its axis, eternal, true, despotic, nebulous time. Our minimal amount will slip across that unfinished bridge, which no architectonic imagination has managed to foresee.

transitive

It had always been incredibly difficult for him to clearly grasp the idea of time. A moment came when he did not know if it was April or June, without being certain of the year either. One beautiful day he noticed the tree in the yard had sprouted buds

overnight. It seemed to display remarkable punctu-
ality – despite the artifices of the city's haze – where
he was so often mistaken. He considered it opportune
to learn a calendrical lesson. He watched the tree at
all hours and since he found such a variety of entertaining manifestations in its motionlessness, he began
spending longer and longer intervals absorbed in
its examination. A moment finally came when it
discovered it was being observed in its stillness by an
old man behind dusty windows who cast his quiet,
empty, inclement eyes on its branches.

turtle

> ... *and lighted / the little O, the Earth.*
> William Shakespeare

The speedy turtle now placed in orbit
looks down – is there any doubt? –
to disdain the slow world,
a speck asleep in its routine,
there on the ground of night
revolving in its calm,
as if it were possible to forget
that in the lagoons of the high heavens,
I, the turtle, rule alone.

U

unicorn

    The narwhal has the glory of its horn
    – unbelievable size, spiraling shape –
    and the uneasy suspicion it's strange,
    not knowing if it's hell or heaven born.

    A ruse raised in museums to adorn
    corners with ivory, a winter shade,
    forging its legend with each passing age
    as it whitens, the timeless unicorn.

    The narwhal through true waters navigates,
    with no one to safeguard its future breath.
    Meanwhile, in waters our dream activates,

    the unicorn stands firm and millenary:
    light's paladin battling against death,
    unfazed by the real, the imaginary.

unpredictability

Happy are the unpredictable. They will be the hell of others.

V

vacant lots

    So very precious, they appear in the path of our childhood wandering. They freely offer their field of illusions that allots ground and sky, insects and grasses, and that minute of coveted freedom welcomes a more felicitous sun to its irradiant green space for the adventure of stumbling, of the imaginary discovery. Because we were unearthing unknown edible species, life-saving when war came along with its shortages, of which we had already received word. Also the beauty of the red castor plant, the spot to dig for treasure, a limb from the tree of tears and laughter, a rabbit-fur glove, a tiny wooden clog. It was all interrupted by the urgent call to wake up, but the heart again embraces that tiny, innocent kingdom in memories, where we speak with a white soothing tongue that tastes of fennel, unassuming anise, our lone discovery.

vagrant

    They sleep during the day, untroubled by the light, by the people who walk past pretending not to see them. One is young, stocky, slightly reddish blond hair. You might say he is the 'homeowner' and the other, older, has come round to visit. The young one has the luxury of a cat, tied with a rope, not too long, around its waist, a lustrous black cat, well fed, with a red collar, like a house cat that had its own cushion, fireplace, the closed bedroom that they prefer in winter. While its master sleeps, it sleeps nestled against his stomach, like a public proclamation of the comfort of its domain. The three of them perfectly occupy the dimensions of the grating that vents the warm air rising from the boilers in the adjacent building. That warmth creates, on this street corner open to the four winds, the space they inhabit. It has no visible limits but, over the days, these have been created to the point that when I pass through there during one of the rare moments when their place is empty, I involuntarily adjust my course so as not to invade the privacy floating in the air. When both are home, if not sleeping, they are talking. Oftentimes assisted by a bottle of red wine. About what, calm, persistent? You never see them reading newspapers, they have no transistor radio. Around noon they leave their space, which, to be exact, is at Lhomond and Ulm. They are no doubt eating, someplace where they have heard about things that nourish besides the chat in which they are engaged. In our eyes, we who live with so many almost sacred objects that condition us, they flamboyantly dispense with everything, just like they dispense with privacy. They do not hide their sleep, their do-nothingness, their scratching, their relationship with the frugal frontiers of that cube of warm air, sufficient solitude for them amid an immoderate world. They do not answer the phone, they have no books and keep no records, they do not cling to provisions and previsions, to clothing to don on different occasions. There is an ordinary hat I sometimes see on the head of one, but it can show up on the head of the other.

Paris has, it seems, a pact with its *clochards*. Every so often it collects them, bathes them, cuts their hair, covers their innocence with old clothes. They are not, then, so detached from their fellow citizens. A man entering the Foyer Libanais with an armful of baguettes has given them one. And I have seen the redhead play for hours on end with a beautiful dog that likely belongs to some neighbor, inventing different tricks to keep it there a little longer. At night, because of the wine or stimulated by the silence of the neighborhood at rest, the voices of the two sedentary vagrants grow excited, rising, also warm, up to the window where from time to time we glance out at them, like at the tree that this particular corner does not have: an ash, a chestnut, a sycamore. We leave as spring's first green splendors are bursting forth anywhere they can. Among other flowerings, we will miss those of our two friends, now as bare as winter trees, when they too receive their portion of the new resurrection's smile.

W

war

Nothing announces the commotion in the pale dusk
of autumn, whose sky displays no other conflict but
one between colors, when a childlike pink modulating
to lilac tries to prevail over the light blue, which in
the end fades to an anodyne white. However, the
long rumble that reaches us from who knows where
startles the first time, concerns on repetition, a second
and a third time, at brief and irregular intervals.
Explosions in the city? They sound more like cannon
fire. It is strange. Austin has kept us removed from
certain fears that are the horrific daily bread of so
many places; we only expect the commotion, also
concerning, of fire alarms – fortunately almost always
false – and ambulances demanding we clear the way.

All the birds that have already taken flight, like
every evening, punctual when the time comes to settle
into their trees, carry out a frightened about-face and
head, visibly indecisive, toward the southern hills in
the direction opposite the source of the noise, muted
and muffled, that is repeated twice more. Friday,
Saturday, and Sunday... three days when at sunset

the mysterious enemy fires its three punctual cannon blasts and retreats into the ensuing silence, inside the tenuous vapors exuded by the city, toward some depression on the horizon, between tree-covered hills. On Monday the resounding booms have dissipated and the mystery is no more. There is war, yes, there are cannon blasts, yes, but they contain only gunpowder: the enemy is the grackle. The intention is not to kill them (that would trigger a commotion among nature's defenders, who are quite a few) but rather to divert them from one of their habitual locations, the university. Is it so serious? They are accused of taking over all the trees on campus, which for some time now undeniably smells of chicken coop. The birds are also early risers and their enthusiastic and multifarious songs have imposed a waking schedule on the student residences that begins well before the one required for courses. And between student discontent and grackles, the choice is clear.

As newcomers to Austin, when we surveyed its natural charms, the squirrels and grackles offered their visible and prolific existence. It was not yet that radiant time of the mockingbird; the robin and the gorgeous bluebird, similar to the cardinal in shape and crest but whose plumage shares the blue spectrum of certain Persian ceramics, have a shorter stay or are more skittish or more autumnal. It was indeed in early autumn when I witnessed the grace of an entire flock, brown mantles and rust-colored breasts, as they descended upon a tree to rest during their migration south; they devoured the tiny red berries on the nearby holly, unfrightened by our presence. After a week they continued on their journey, their strength replenished, the berries consumed, or prompted by their inner clock. Months later, I picked up a beautiful little bird the size of a sparrow, its delicate down an incandescent yellow, a summer visitor: a male yellow-breasted kiskadee, I believe. Intact, he had fallen in mid-flight. I left him on the ground in a flowerbed. In India, during ancient times, birds of prey took care of the dead. Ants are no less ritualistic nor less swift. On my way back soon after, there were hundreds of them busied with their task.

We live along a migratory route. Many other birds have certainly passed through; they slip by me, faster or more inconspicuous, although I cannot rule out the possibility that climatic vagaries have something to do with my decreased observations. Such encounters do not happen every day because many birds avoid populated areas. Birdwatchers must communicate with one another, be ready, rigorous, and patient in order to achieve their observations. One time we joined a couple of these platonic onlookers. We had to travel several kilometers to the environs of Lake Buchanan so that, on a particular path in the middle of nowhere, identical to any other as far as I could tell, we kept our extraordinary appointment with a pair of flycatchers, she salmon red, he fire red. The two hunters, face to face, each in their own tree, would swoop down on unsuspecting insects and return to the same spot as if attached by an invisible elastic band. We beheld that arboreal *pas de deux* for half an hour. When we left them, if by some chance we had found that spectacle to be lacking, nature completed it for us: we saw a scuttling armadillo, as large as a pig, as nimble as a jackrabbit. Also, as we were crossing through fields, we noticed a solitary horse in the distance. He came toward us, eager for company. We were able to greet him with several crackers. When we climbed into the car to leave, he placed his head on the trunk and looked at us with his loving eyes. Few humans are as demonstrative when we leave them. There was peace and tenderness in him.

Getting back to the grackles, today their colony has again prospered, so well that I am preparing myself for the second offensive against them. When night falls, if I am at home, I know I will stop whatever I am doing for a few minutes to watch the rambunctious, fast-moving cloud that always comes from the same point and passes diagonally over our corner, proceeding mysteriously beyond it to occupy specific trees on three or four blocks of Guadalupe Street.

wind

When when when when when?
How how how how?
What for what for what for?

window

Through the Ark's lone window (it must have had more for the respiration of so many animals and to better decorate the three floors that Jehovah required), Noah saw the return of the celebrated branch-beaked dove, more explanatory than the raven. Through the windows of high towers overlooking the sea, one caught sight of catastrophes of legend, the beloved who drowns in his attempt to conquer distances, the black sails that Theseus has forgotten to change. Through its great number of windows, Homer tells us, indirectly, of the magnificence of Priam's palace. '*En la mar hay una torre / en la torre una ventana / en la ventana hay una niña / que a los marineros llama*'

(In the sea there is a tower / In the tower there is a window / In the window there is a girl / Who calls out to the sailors): because it comes from Sepharad, I have slightly adjusted the beginning of this song to Castilian, its charm for me lying not only in the melody, which I feel watching over me; also in its approach by degrees to the central girl, through a spyglass adjusting its focus. Sea, tower, and window: steps equal in value. Medieval engravings eternalize an anxious maiden beneath an ogive – sometimes disproportionately large, as if she were the size of her solitude – while she looks in vain toward the road on which the crusader has yet to return. But if the maiden grows impatient, the window can also give way to the temptations she might wish to allow herself. This is how the troubadour's song gained entry, and although he supposedly sang of impossible love, perhaps his body did also, covetous of a more hushed rhythm. In the background of a Flemish painting, what the window lets us see sings in counterpoint with the protagonistic figures in the foreground. They sometimes fade from our memory, but the music coming from the painting's distant views continues singing for us with soft colors, skies, and trees.

If the Ark was lacking in windows, Álvaro Cunqueiro, an imaginative and erudite fabulist, tells us of the Turpian Tower, also lacking but in doors. There were none, at least none that were visible. There was a black dwarf at the windowsill, lowering an enchanted ladder of clouds down to those who deserved to ascend it. Windows were interesting, living elements and could offer unexpected emotions. I remember the ones in the Episcopal Palace of Astorga, an unfinished work by Gaudí. They reached the floor and seemed not to have foreseen a need for bars or some other form of protection against the openness. Not a sufficient believer in divine providence, a distrustful archbishop ordered its access be suspended. This is how I saw it.

Today, when monotonous masses can be or appear to be nothing but windows, the window has lost its power. 'Seventy balconies and not one flower,' lamented Baldomero Fernández Moreno. They no longer think of flowers, neither these towers nor those who hardly inhabit them. From my window I can see one hundred and eighty-two windows with their balconies, and not one ripple of leaves in the wind brings me hope that inside that luxury anthill someone is thinking about the future of the earth, each day more cadaverous.

X

Xanthippe

I am grateful to history or legend for preserving the memory of Xanthippe, through the mediation of Plato and Xenophon, even if it has been to execrate her. So many consorts have been forgotten, cast aside, over the course of the centuries... It would almost be normal for us not to know anything about her at all, given the only knowledge we have of Socrates' father and mother are their (obviously metaphorical) professions: a sculptor and a midwife respectively. We even have very diverse images of Socrates himself, though according to Cicero he was the one who called philosophy down from the heavens to the earth, introducing it into homes and the market. Along the way something may have grazed Xanthippe.

The plebian Socrates – in Nietzsche's view – had a fittingly plebeian Xanthippe. It is possible that she was a bit stubborn and no softer to the touch than pig bristles. In Xenophon's *Symposium*, Antisthenes considers her to be the most unpleasant woman of all time. Like the horse trainer who prefers to begin with an ill-tempered animal, if her husband were able to tolerate her, his relations with the rest of humanity would be easier. We know almost nothing of her life, but the passage in which she empties a pot of water over Socrates' head has spanned almost fifteen centuries. Did she realize he was below the window or was it chance that wronged him in the precise moment when, like any Athenian woman, she was meticulously cleaning her house? In this virulence enduring for so long, nobody thinks about the wife's rights, obviously reduced by the philosopher's pedagogical Eros. I believe this scene has nothing to do with him or with her. If human beings are the work they leave behind, Socrates, who did not leave a single line of his own, is in words a fiction, mostly by Plato. But so too is the viper's bite on the souls who got near him and on Athenian society, told to pursue – and not betray – the truth. One day Athenian society, like other democracies that modeled themselves after it, irrevocably punished the person who wished to cure them, later regretting it and punishing his accusers.

The thoughtful Socrates, bound in my mind to that 'rooster for Asclepius' (faintly dissonant for so long), in his resigned flight from the world seems to compromise his ill-tempered wife, leaving her, for many, in debtor's fraud. The bitter Nietzsche will be who unintentionally bestows her with her greatest merit: her bad personality causes Socrates to seek out the streets and in them his disciples and to discover dialectics.

Without a doubt, his undisputed irony relied on the figure of his special companion. He may have thought that part of the dismembered union is always chosen to be deemed in the right. In that magic square with Socrates at its center, Xanthippe represents the angle of everyday life as much as does Xenophon, whose portrait of the philosopher is more human and realistic than the almost divine image depicted by Plato. The latter occupies another angle, and the other is Diotima, the foreigner from Mantinea, Apollo's hierophant servant. The ugly Socrates meets her during his search for *aletheia*, for the hidden truth, and she will propose he find beauty in itself. Was Xanthippe able to understand this? The poor woman disappears from history when her philosopher, the hemlock hour at hand, has her remove herself from the prison so that her feminine weeping does not disturb his serenity.

Xenophon, in his *Memorabilia*, at least rescues her as a mother.

Y

yuyo

    For *y*, such a noble and Greek letter, which some call Pythagorean because Pythagoras derived a morality from the bifurcation of its two ascending strokes, I offer a beloved Spanish word, humble like the one that dictionaries give as a synonym: *yerbajo* (weed). But I am unwilling to apply this pejorative verdict to something minimized by our ignorance: there is a reason for all things in nature, even if we do not find it in what disturbs us or seems not to be to our advantage. The unpretentious plant, if limited in aesthetic virtues, is perhaps not so in chemical benefits. And make no mistake, in the natural chain it must be useful to some creature, however tiny.

    Many times, I have gone too far, casually applying it to any little plant whose name I did not know, aware that my *yeísmo* also added to the perplexity and maybe the discredit (of the word and my own).

    While not many words starting with *y* captivate me (what to do with the abusive first-person *yo*?), there are indeed many names deserving of attention, like Yates, that illuminating monster of fascinating erudition, and pseudonyms like that giant of French literature, Yourcenar, and the richly complex William Butler Yeats, and those strange saints or mystics or lunatics, the Japanese Yamabushi, who slowly commit suicide by dehydration, imagining that this brings them closer to purity, and what better state than that to enter death?

Z

z

Unfortunate is the letter z, and not because it rests in the final foothills of the dictionary or because of the stabbing lightning bolt zigzag that depicts it or because of the hexes Barthes attributes to it as a letter of deviation, a deviant letter: because we remember it little more than to denigrate things: Z movies. We feel it takes too long to reach to refer to a simplicity, preferring instead the elementary 'ABC'. It was better off as zeta in Greek, closer at hand in sixth place. I had concluded this review (initiated on a whim decades ago and whose ragbag nature guaranteed its peaceful and undemanding survival among the things that can wait), when a new impulse put it in order and completed it, I discovered I had very unjustifiably neglected the z. Zounds! In recent years, haphazard ones, I briefly heard *zorzales* (thrushes), but discovered *zanates* (rooks), iridescently azure, which reappeared later in Austin as graceful grackles and continued kindling my zoolatry. I also discovered the delight of the *zapote* (sapote) and celebrated a city – Zacatecas – with hidden corners, cloisters, a clear and high sky, endearing kindness. For all these reasons, my oversight was abhorrent. I tried to right my injustice once the idea of an alphabetical arrangement had lost some of its virginity (Alberto Savinio's *Nuova Enciclopedia* appeared around 1970 and there was even a novel whose sections progressed according to this order), and I decided to begin bringing this almost secret vice to a close, this maze of diverse texts. It led me to a distant impression, dormant but not opaque inside me; and with this zeppelin that came flying along, I will begin to take my leave, on to another book, I trust, if I can find hands in which to leave this one.

zeppelin

Without a doubt, it warranted the unexpected. That she be taken from her bed, asleep, and that someone – it was Uncle Pericles – carry her in his arms up the steep iron staircase to the mezzanine and from there, up one more, wooden and short, at the end of which he had to stoop down to cross beneath the low lintel of the door leading to the rooftop terrace. Wrapped in her blanket, inside the fog of deep childhood sleep, she hardly grasped just how unusual such maneuvers were. The roof was not a place for gatherings, particularly at night, since one had to traverse the dominions of the housekeeper, whose privacy, however modest, was respected. But the girl, having discovered in those summits a limitless domain for her mental adventures, at least for some of them, clambered up whenever she could. Had the house caught fire? Were they fleeing upward? She did not have much time for imagination. In the sky, profoundly blue and starry, the full moon conceded its splendor to an enormous, peaceful, ovate balloon resembling an enchanted silver soup tureen that, without its feet, had ascended with the steam of its contents. It passed over the sleeping houses as if it were marching through eternity, with gentle slowness, quiet like a dream. It moved through a field unknown to those who watched it; from its observable luminosity flowed such an absence of sound that the awe-struck silence below was almost as majestic as the one above, and it rose magnetized by it, both dispensing with any human presences. The ribbon of their gazes was being woven and unwoven in an act that would have no continuation and even less future. The girl found herself before a world of ghosts bidding farewell. Beside her they talked about this arrival, this freedom, between lethal and magical, like a passage that was never going to be repeated. With time, she met someone who had seen Halley's Comet cross the sky in his youth and hoped to live long enough to again witness its periodic appearance over the Earth, or at least to still count himself among the living on that date. Human and not celestial, the zeppelin did not accept pending appointments nor allow sentimental exorcisms and, unaware of its fiery destiny, the only ending worthy of that fairy-tale moment, it floated into the distance against a curtain of blue and black, a Diana's Tree planted, which the night uses to set its ceremonial stage – decked out in black? – toward the shelf of great memories: the night the zeppelin flew over Montevideo.

zuibitsu

The asymmetry, the freedom, the independence of a text in relation to others, the mixture of prose and poetry, rival governesses, each one on her own shore, does not trouble me nor cause me more thirst than it should. I believe the differing tones could ultimately become a pleasant virtue. There is a species of mimosa tree that mixes distinct types of leaves in its crown when it blooms, offering them in a single bouquet, and it never crosses our mind that nature has constructed some kitschy idyll by harboring this union of differences. There was a time when still lifes were in fashion, *natures mortes*, vases bursting with diverse flowers against a dark backdrop. I saw an enormous gallery covered with them in a museum that was stunning though in crisis. I like the style of these paintings, but the repetition embedded in a single moment tries my patience. The presence of distinct and even discordant lines in a book promotes fragmentariness, a quality that any admirer of Lichtenberg will find commendable, although I admit that this alone does not make rain and fine weather. Many years back, I wanted to organize and lighten my folders. In that feminine spirit of putting leftovers to good use that has created so many delicious recipes or those magnificent patchworks by American pioneers, I thought it was perhaps possible to find a magnet that would unite scattered filings and attract others. For a long period of time during which infinite things also took place, I reveled in the collecting of heterogeneous particles not opposed to living together. I did not have the slightest idea I was reproducing a *zuibitsu* or *zuihit su*, 'follow-the-brush', an ancient Japanese literary form that gathers assorted matters, anecdotes, delights, musings, judgments, etc. Still more time had to pass to come across an example in the peaceful reflections of Kenko.

There is no shortage of warnings for humility, for our proper position in the world, and they come from many places, even from me. How can I not faithfully acknowledge the little land left to me by the prodigious creative joy of those who came before from so many places to invent almost everything for us, even literary genres?

'Well, now that we *have* seen each other,'
said the Unicorn, 'if you'll believe in me,
I'll believe in you…'

CHARCO PRESS

Director & Editor: Carolina Orloff
Director: Samuel McDowell

www.charcopress.com

Lexicon of Affinities was published on
80gsm Munken Premium Cream paper.

The text was designed using Bembo 11.5 and ITC Galliard.

Printed in August 2024 by TJ Books
Padstow, Cornwall, PL28 8RW using responsibly
sourced paper and environmentally-friendly adhesive.